She wasn't going to fall for Rafe.

Not again. She was way too smart for that.

He broke the silence. "I...I should go."

"Yes." Jordan took a deep breath. "But thank you for your help tonight. I must have seemed out of control. That's not the real me."

He canted his head. "You were fine. It's completely understandable."

"I'm sure you've never lost your cool like over something so...*replaceable*."

"A few times, actually."

"I have a difficult time believing it."

"All *things* are replaceable. But not people."

She wanted to believe that, but he'd replaced *her*, with Liz. It had only taken him a few weeks, too. And it hurt to this day to realize how expendable she'd been. How quickly he'd moved on.

He stopped in the doorframe, just inches from her. "Jordan, *look at me*."

Reluctantly, she raised her eyes to meet his gaze. "Yes?"

"You're not replaceable. And I missed the hell out of you." With that, he turned and walked out the door without a backward glance.

Dear Reader,

Welcome back to Charming, Texas! You're all invited to a wedding. Event planner extraordinaire Jordan Del Toro wants everything about her older brother's wedding to be perfect but she's already starting with one strike against her. Her ex, and Max's oldest friend, Rafe, is part of the wedding party. He will attend, along with his precocious daughter, Susan.

They're thrown together for a family wedding, which might just be a little bit awkward. Something always goes wrong in a wedding, and Jordan is battling more than her feelings this time. At the time I began to write this book, my own granddaughter was Susan's age. Coincidence? I think not. Every day I took notes and kept track of all the cute things "Bean" would say and do. Someday maybe she'll even read this book (many, many years from now if I have anything to say about it).

Thanks again to my amazing readers for all suggestions of things that go wrong at a wedding. There were so many, some that I didn't even use. As always, I love to hear from you. Drop me a line anytime at heatherly@heatherlybell.com. If you want to keep in touch, sign up for my newsletter.

Heatherly

A Charming Single Dad

HEATHERLY BELL

HARLEQUIN
SPECIAL
EDITION

Recycling programs
for this product may
not exist in your area.

ISBN-13: 978-1-335-72465-6

A Charming Single Dad

Copyright © 2023 by Heatherly Bell

For questions and comments about the quality of this book,
please contact us at CustomerService@Harlequin.com.

Harlequin Enterprises ULC
22 Adelaide St. West, 41st Floor
Toronto, Ontario M5H 4E3, Canada
www.Harlequin.com

Printed in U.S.A.

Bestselling author **Heatherly Bell** was born in Tuscaloosa, Alabama, but lost her accent by the time she was two. After leaving Alabama, Heatherly lived with her family in Puerto Rico and Maryland before being transplanted kicking and screaming to the California Bay Area. She now loves it here, she swears. Except the traffic.

Books by Heatherly Bell

Harlequin Special Edition

Charming, Texas

Winning Mr. Charming
The Charming Checklist
A Charming Christmas Arrangement

The Fortunes of Texas: Hitting the Jackpot

Winning Her Fortune

Montana Mavericks:
The Real Cowboys of Bronco Heights

Grand-Prize Cowboy

Wildfire Ridge

More than One Night
Reluctant Hometown Hero
The Right Moment

Visit the Author Profile page
at Harlequin.com for more titles.

In memory of my father, Carlos Antonio Font,
and for fathers everywhere who love their children
and do the best they can.

Chapter One

Rafe Reyes woke when something very wet and cold touched his nose. His wake-up call was usually his daughter Susan's little finger jabbing him awake.

He blinked and rubbed his eyes, and a big ball of golden fur tried to French-kiss him.

"Bleh!" Rafe sat up, rubbing saliva off his mouth.

"Oh, he's so *cute*." Susan giggled. "Sub loves you. He gave you a kiss!"

"He gave me a slobber."

Susan stood by his bedside, still wearing her Little Mermaid pajamas. Her dimpled smile and bright blue eyes never failed to tug a smile out of him. He'd need to do something about her hair today. Blond waves swirled around her face and tangled at her shoulders. Pigtails today? Maybe braids. He'd become an expert at both.

She bent to hug Yellow Submarine, a Labrador retriever and her new best friend. From the moment she'd met him yesterday, they'd been inseparable. Sub, for short, had appointed himself Susan's shadow.

"I want to go to the beach. I want to take Sub! He can chase me, and we can build castles."

The cobwebs in Rafe's brain slowly began to unfurl. Oh, yeah, he'd promised her the beach today.

"Okay, baby. Give Daddy a minute to put a shirt on."

He and Susan were staying in the converted lighthouse belonging to Cole Kinsella, who had been a navy SEAL and served in the same team as Rafe's best friend, Max Del Toro. Cole and his wife, Valerie, had been kind enough to put him and Susan up. Coming to Charming for Max's wedding week meant Rafe had pulled Susan out of preschool for a couple of weeks, causing yet another argument with Liz. But it was summer, and the first time he'd had a visitation with Susan for this long since the divorce. He didn't see any harm in their daughter enjoying a stay in the small, bucolic Texas Gulf Coast town.

This was the first vacation he'd had in years, and a welcome break from life in the big city of Dallas. He detested city living but Liz had a good job with a defense contractor firm. They'd moved to Texas from Atlanta, where she'd formerly been stationed, in one last attempt to save their crumbling marriage.

Rafe pulled a T-shirt over his head. "Last one to the kitchen is a rotten egg!"

Because every day he tried to be the father Susan deserved, Rafe gave her a head start. Sub didn't need one as he bounded down the steps ahead of them both. Susan skipped down the winding staircase that had been repurposed from an old ship, holding on to the rail.

Rafe was still in a state of amazement caused by the converted lighthouse. Upstairs on the outdoor deck, an old-fashioned telescope made it possible to get a spectacular view of the gulf. There were portholes for windows, a modern kitchen and a living room with one of Cole's old surfboards serving as a coffee table. Wood floors gleamed. Nautical themes were everywhere, but one might expect this from the home of a surfing enthusiast and former SEAL.

On the landing, Rafe swept Susan up in his arms. "Somebody didn't get her morning tickle!"

Susan dissolved in a flurry of squeals and laughter, trying her best to get away from the tickle monster. The kitchen was still quiet; no sign of Cole or Valerie awake.

He set Susan's wiggling body down. "What do you want for breakfast?"

"Pancakes!" Susan twirled around the kitchen. "With chocolate chips!"

Rafe had been told to make himself at home. During his stay, he planned to be indispensable to the couple expecting their first child. They had saved him hundreds of dollars on a hotel room. His merely adequate salary as a Dallas firefighter and paramedic didn't allow much for extras like vacations in coastal beach towns.

Making his hosts breakfast seemed like a good place to start paying back the favor.

"Good idea. Even Cole and Valerie will appreciate my chocolate chip pancakes." He got busy looking through cabinets for a pan, flour and ingredients. "Do you want to help?"

"Of course, I'm a great helper."

Zero lack of confidence in this one. Then again, she parroted nearly everything he said. He'd learned early on that kids came with no subterfuge or filter. For this reason, and many others, he watched what he said in her presence.

"You *are* a great helper." Rafe cracked an egg into the bowl and handed her a spoon to stir.

"When I was a little girl, I didn't know how to do this but now I'm old, so I know."

He smirked. "Yes, Susan. You're old now."

She meant *older*, of course, but her four-year-old conversational skills were still developing when it came to time. It wasn't quite linear to her.

"Mommy's old. And *you're* old."

Rafe might only be thirty-three, but he sometimes felt ten years older. Susan had utterly domesticated him, which he figured had everything to do with it. He was the weekend dad who filled his days with his daughter, taking her to parks and museums.

Other than his work for the Dallas Fire Department, and Susan, he had no life. He didn't date. Sadly, he'd become boring. But he hadn't planned on being a divorced single dad at his age. He'd had no plans to marry, either. And when he'd pictured marriage, someday, it was only to the woman he'd loved for half his life.

But you blew that possibility to smithereens.

Yeah, best not to think about Jordan Del Toro. He'd see her soon enough, which would be as pleasant as a root canal without anesthesia and hurt twice as much.

Susan was still working on her first pancake, light eater that she was, while Rafe had already consumed three. Valerie and Cole came down the staircase a few minutes later, visible from the kitchen due to the open floor plan and vaulted ceilings.

"Good morning, you two," Valerie said, mussing Susan's hair.

Cole fist-bumped with Rafe. "You didn't have to do all this."

"My pleasure. As my daughter will tell you, I'm the pancake whisperer."

"*Chocolate chip* pancakes?" Valerie said. "Ever since I got pregnant, I've been craving chocolate. I think I love you."

"No, you don't." Cole hooked an arm around his bride. "You love *me*."

"I was talking to the pancake, but I would love you

even more if you'd cook me anything with chocolate."
She gave him a quick kiss.

Rafe would have given his left heart ventricle to
have had this kind of a marriage. But contrary to
some cultural and religious beliefs, love didn't necessarily grow because two people were committed
to each other. It didn't take root and flourish because
those two people were compatible and desperately
wanted to make their family work. Rafe had learned
the hard way that you couldn't help whom you loved.
He and Liz had done their best to give Susan the
home she deserved, but in the end they'd failed mis-
erably. He'd managed to be a good father, but he'd
done a poor job as Liz's husband.

"What are your plans today?" Rafe asked, hand-
ing them both a plate of pancakes. "I promised Susan
the beach."

"Can we please take Sub with us?" Susan piped
in. "He really loves me."

"Sure can. Sub loves the beach." Cole said. "I'll
go with you guys. I haven't surfed for a week."

"I'm going to the dress fitting," Valerie said, covering her pancake with syrup. "This is going to be
a disaster. Ava has us wearing strapless dresses."

"What's wrong with that?" Rafe asked.

"Well, I'm a lot bigger than normal. *Everywhere*."

"Don't worry, Jordan has this all under control,"
Cole said. "If she has to sew brand-new dresses for
y'all I have no doubt she would do it."

"Tell her I said hello," Rafe said, knowing Jordan

would be a lot more receptive to a secondhand greeting through Valerie.

"Why don't you take Valerie?" Cole suggested. "That way you can say hello yourself."

Ah, Cole was taking pity on Rafe. Kind of him. "Thanks, but I told Susan we'd hit the beach."

"I can do that," Cole said.

"No surfing." Valerie pointed. "Taking care of Susan will be good practice for you."

"We'll chase waves and build sandcastles," Cole said.

"Is that okay with you?" Rafe tipped his daughter's chin up to meet his gaze.

"I'm not a baby anymore. Sub will take care of me."

Cole splayed his hands. "Hey, what about me? Why do I always lose to Sub?"

"*Cole* will take care of you," Rafe corrected. "He's in charge. When he tells you to do something, you'll do it. Are we clear?"

Susan bobbed her head up and down. "Yeah, bro. I got it."

Cole burst into laughter and fist-bumped Susan. "Genius."

"I'll go take a shower and get ready," Rafe said.

At least he'd see Jordan Del Toro for the first time in a public setting where if she wanted to draw and quarter him, she'd be forced to reconsider.

Still, he hadn't been this nervous since the day he'd come home to tell Jordan he'd be marrying someone else.

* * *

Jordan Del Toro handled chaos, and weddings were her specialty. Weddings were 80 percent of her event planning business, Jordan Makes Plans, and she'd seen some…stuff. There was this one time when guests had thought it cute to blow bubbles toward the bride and groom as they entered the reception hall. But it had rained the night before, making the wood deck slick enough for a bride wearing three-inch heels to nearly slip and fall. Thankfully, the groom had moved fast enough to hold up the bride. Crisis averted.

Then there was the bridesmaid Jordan had found outside the reception venue, passed out drunk, her left boob hanging out of the *strapless* dress. Jordan had helped provide coverage while the girl shoved the boob back into place, then led the bridesmaid to the ladies' room so she could splash water on her face. She'd pumped her full of coffee. Crisis averted.

Yet another time, the groom was found making out with the maid of honor. Crisis *not* averted. She couldn't win them all.

But for the wedding of her older brother, Max, to Ava Long, every crisis would be averted. She had experience. She had chutzpah. She had skills.

She had two senior citizens insisting that there be a poetry reading in place of a first dance.

"I've written a poem for Max and Ava that they will adore," Patsy Villanueva said. "It's quite romantic, if I do say so myself, and I've censored some of the spicier details since children will be present."

"Instead of erotic poetry, I suggest quoting from the classics. Perhaps Shakespeare. Or Emily Dickinson. She was a true romantic." This was from Etta May Virgil, president of the local senior citizen poetry group named the Almost Dead Poet Society.

Yes, they had a president.

"Emily Dickinson?" Patsy shook her head. "Poor woman. I suggest Jane Austen. Perhaps something from *Emma*? Or *Pride and Prejudice*?"

"Jane Austen was not a *poet*," Etta May said.

"I beg to differ," said Patsy.

Jordan took a sip of the strong brew supplied by Ava's coffee company and served by the Salty Dog Bar & Grill. Her brother and two of his best friends owned and ran the place where she now sat and tried to relax before her appointments today.

"All sound like wonderful ideas," Jordan lied. "I'll run them by Ava just as soon as I can."

"See?" Mrs. Villanueva elbowed Etta May. "I knew she'd listen."

Waving, they both went back to their booth.

Jordan had arrived late last night to Charming, Texas, from her home in Santa Cruz, California, two weeks before the wedding. Because for the first time in her career, she'd planned a wedding *long-distance*. Also for the first time, she was a bridesmaid *and* wedding planner. The rest of the Del Toro clan would arrive next week, but she was far too much of a control freak not to be present ahead of time. Everything would go according to her carefully laid plans. She'd arrived early enough to anticipate, and avert, any crisis. This was her brother's wedding, after all, and *nothing* could go wrong. It had to be perfect.

She told herself it was her constant desire to achieve utter perfection that was making her anxious, and not the thought of seeing Rafe for the first time in four years.

Jordan consulted the leather planner that rarely left her presence. Old-school, sure, but it worked for her. She was a tactile and visual person to the nth degree. To that end, she'd planned nearly every minute of the fourteen days she'd be in Charming. Final cake testing, dress fitting, picking up wedding favors, caterer details, videographer and flowers. A trip to the beach had been scheduled in or her sister Maribel would accuse her of being a workaholic. By her calculations, this left zero minutes to reconnect, or otherwise chat, with Rafe. There would be no small talk or "happy" reunion.

She would say a quick hello to both his daughter and wife, Liz, and Rafe, too, since it could not be avoided, and stay busy every second until Geoff Costner arrived. Geoff, her attorney boyfriend extraordinaire of two years, happened to be the best plus-one a woman could ever hope for. He was handsome, a great flirt, knew how to dance and was going to make Rafe rue the day.

Both her present and future looked bright, and

soon enough she'd marry Geoff. They were perfect for each other, as all his colleagues continually reminded them. A month ago, he'd suggested they get married rather than continue to live in separate condos. He was right, of course, and even if it wasn't the most romantic proposal, it certainly was the most practical.

Since he hadn't officially asked, she'd simply told him sure, it was a good idea. Then she'd waited for a ring, or something a little more…romantic. When it didn't come, she realized that Geoff just wasn't the type. It would be up to her as the organizer half of the couple to firm up details and choose a date. He was a good man. Sure, he lacked skills in the romance department, but she could do without those. Romantic and passionate men tended to be over the top and, more often than not, their fervor burned itself out. Been there, done that. She was a lot smarter now.

"Sorry we're late." Ava bustled up to the booth, two older women in tow. She took a seat across from Jordan. "Jordan, this is my mother, Dr. Katherine Long, and Lucia Perez, the woman who helped raise me."

Dr. Long resembled her daughter, but contrary to the always colorful Ava, was dressed in a classy black monochrome pantsuit. The matronly woman, Ava's former nanny and practically a member of the family, had beautiful latte skin and short salt-and-pepper hair. She wore a bright, multicolored skirt and matching top. From the beginning, Jordan had asked enough questions of Ava to know that they were basically dealing with not one mother of the bride, but *two*.

"Are you both attending the cake testing?" Jordan consulted her planner. This was the first appointment today, but she didn't have a note in that regard.

"Is that a problem?" Dr. Long exchanged a look with Lucia. "We had both planned for this."

"Of course not," Jordan said, snapping her book shut. "The more the merrier."

"*Ay, muy bueno*, I came all the way from Colombia," Lucia said in her thick accent. "What a special time this is."

"They both just want to be a part of our day," Ava said, her usual bubbly self.

Jordan had first met her future sister-in-law when she visited the Del Toro family in Watsonville, California, last Christmas. There was no way anyone could meet the effervescent Ava Long and not instantly like her. The only surprise was that someone as grumpy and uptight as her former navy SEAL brother had wound up with a Miss Sunshine.

"Would anyone like some coffee first or should we get going?" Jordan glanced at her Fitbit watch.

Efficient, because it gave her the time, how many steps she'd taken in a day and her heart rate. That last one was important because Jordan fully expected it to blow into the triple digits, and for the first time, not due to a difficult bride.

"We had coffee at the hotel," Dr. Long explained.

"And I skipped breakfast so that I could eat as many samples as possible."

"I'm ready when you are," Ava said. "First, cake testing. Next, dress fittings."

Jordan climbed out of the booth. "We should get going. I like to be early."

Early or on time were the only timelines on Jordan's radar. She'd said goodbye to her carefree ways long ago.

Chapter Two

Not every wedding planner attended bridal fittings, but not only was this a family affair, Jordan also overstressed about strapless dresses after the bridesmaid's boobage fiasco. And Ava had chosen a royal blue strapless bridesmaid dress, though she had one bridesmaid who was six months pregnant. To say Jordan was *concerned* would be putting it mildly. It definitely wasn't the most practical idea. If asked, she'd have given her expert opinion. No. Just. No.

After the cake testing, Jordan had arrived early to the only wedding boutique in town and now sat alone, consulting her planner. A typical wedding shop, Charmed, I'm Sure was filled with racks of white gowns and a small pedestal in the center of the room surrounded by three-way mirrors. As part of her due diligence, Jordan had alerted the stylist of her concerns with the strapless dress.

All things considered, the cake testing had gone smoothly earlier. The two "mothers" affectionately slugged it out between four tiers and six tiers. Dr. Long thought four tiers were sufficient. But Lucia insisted there be at least six, because everybody should be allowed to indulge on this special day. Finally, to end the standoff, Jordan had reminded both women that this was Ava's day and her decision.

Not surprisingly, Ava had split the difference and gone with five tiers because she hated the thought of anyone going without.

This wedding would *not* be a small and intimate affair. A local business owner, Ava Long was the daughter of two prominent Dallas-based physicians. Max, for his part, was a former navy SEAL and a leader in their business community. Ava had campaigned to have the wedding in Charming, and as her compromise, agreed her engagement could be announced in all the major high-society venues. She had also agreed to be married in the large banquet hall of The Lookout, the only hotel in Charming, when she would have preferred City Hall and a simple reception at the Salty Dog.

Jordan was grateful for the banquet hall choice and had registered for a hotel room there. Last night, after once more checking the size of the hall and double-checking their booking time, she'd settled into her own room at The Lookout.

Briefly, she'd checked in with Geoff. "Please tell me you've already purchased your plane ticket."

"All taken care of. I had my secretary book it."

"Thank you, honey. This wedding is particularly important to me."

Geoff knew all about Rafe. But he also understood that Rafe was married, with a child, so there was zero jealousy on his part. Jordan wished there was a little pinch. It might feel nice to be wanted and reminded she was special. Geoff often got so caught up in work he'd forget the little things. He'd been involved in pretrial preparation of a civil litigation lawsuit for months and they'd both been neglecting their relationship. It would be good to get away, just the two of them.

Then again, she'd been the one to avoid making plans for their wedding like setting an actual date. She was waiting, she had to admit, for a more formal ask from Geoff. But when Max announced his engagement to Ava, Jordan was reminded that she'd crossed an invisible timeline. It was time to get busy and create the happy balance of work and home life.

Ava waltzed into the boutique, pulling Jordan out of her thoughts. Max was with her.

Jordan stood, crossed her arms and jutted out her hip. "Get *out* of here. It's bad luck for the groom to see the dress."

"Stupid superstition. I'm just dropping off my bride." He kissed Ava, not-so-secretly palmed her butt and then was out the door.

"I hate being apart from him for long, and he'll be in a business meeting the rest of the day," Ava gushed. "This is great, you're all business, and that's exactly what I need right now."

Jordan folded her future sister-in-law into her arms, realizing she'd come off sounding like a shrew. Leave it to Ava to let it go.

"How are you doing with all the excitement? Is it too much?" Jordan asked.

"Oh, no! Are you kidding? I love it!"

"Some brides flip out under all the pressure and anticipation. But this is why Max hired me. I don't want *you* to worry about a single thing. Just enjoy your day. Every detail, and I mean every single detail, is in my book." She then reached for and patted her planner.

"You keep it all in there?"

"Each wedding I do has their own book. Sketches, diagrams, ideas. Details. I'm the most organized person you'll ever meet, which makes me so good at what I do."

"And I *love* that I don't have to worry about a thing."

Just then the doors swung open and a beautiful brunette waltzed in.

"Stacy!" Ava rushed to meet her friend, hugging her as if they hadn't seen each other in decades.

She introduced her to Jordan, and they spent a few minutes getting acquainted.

Stacy wrung her hands together. "I've stopped

breastfeeding my daughter, but honestly? My measurements have um, changed a bit. Hopefully there's enough material to expand."

"Well…" Jordan began.

This could very well be an issue.

"Of course, it's not a problem!" Ava said.

Then again, the bride was always right.

The stylist joined them. "Ava, dear, would you come with me?"

"See you both in a minute!" Ava waved.

Jordan turned to Stacy. "If there's a problem with your dress, we have time for alterations. That's why we're…we're…" Jordan stopped talking when the doors to the shop swung open again.

Valerie Kinsella walked through the open door held by none other than Rafe.

"Hi, there," Valerie said, walking up to them. "Hope y'all don't mind but Rafe wanted to tag along."

Jordan didn't hear any other words. It was as if her world had become a silent movie. Noise became little else but muffled sounds. People talked, their lips moving, and she heard nothing but a buzzing in her ears.

Rafe. This wasn't in her planner.

He wore jeans and a T-shirt, looking so casual that Jordan suddenly felt overdressed in her pink designer jacket dress with black piping. When he stepped in front of her, over four years faded away and she was back home in Watsonville at the fruit stand where Rafe had told her he was marrying Liz.

She'd cried, pulled on him, reminded him that she loved him. Begged him not to marry Liz. In other words, utterly *humiliated* herself in front of this man.

"Jordan?"

She snapped out of it when she found Rafe staring at her curiously, head canted, a slight smile on his lips.

"Oh, hi. Rafe. Yeah. Uh-huh…good to see you again."

He enveloped her into his warm embrace and the walls she'd erected stayed intact. She patted him three times on the back in a friendship sort of way and quickly stepped back.

"I don't know what *you're* doing here. This is all about dresses and fittings. So boring for you, I'm sure."

"Normally. But I wanted to see you."

He sounded sincere. He wanted to see the girl he'd dropped like the stock market crash? Nice of him. Did he expect her to still be wounded and heart-broken? She schooled her features because this was Max's oldest friend and the best man. She'd had every intention of getting along with him, but at the moment she bristled with contempt.

"Well, now you've seen me." She picked up her book and held it to her chest to discourage any more hugging.

"You look good, *cielito lindo.*"

This was his old term of endearment for her,

meaning "pretty sky," and because of those same apparently *poorly* constructed walls, her heart tugged.

"Thanks, and so do you."

Still roguishly handsome, but now there were tiny lines in the corners of his eyes, giving him a mature and worldly look. As always, his very presence upset her equilibrium and threw her back to younger and much weaker times in her life. But even if he'd been her first love, she'd come a long way since Rafe crushed her heart.

She threw a longing look at the bridesmaids, but Stacy and Valerie were engaged in conversation and ignoring everyone else.

And Ava had still not emerged from the dressing room.

Someone please interrupt us. Please. I'm begging you.

When no savior came, she cleared her throat. "So. How are Susan and Liz?"

"Susan is with Cole at the lighthouse. They're going to hang out at the beach. And…well, Liz and I are divorced."

She blinked, completely blindsided. *"Divorced?"*

"That's right."

Why hadn't she known about this? Why hadn't Max told her?

"I'm sorry."

"Don't be. We tried to make it work, for our daughter's sake, and that's all two people who care about each other can do."

Our daughter. Even now the words cut a slice off Jordan's heart. They'd been a little family, at least for a while. It was more than Rafe had ever given her.

"Yes, I guess that's…true."

"How about you? Are you single?"

Jordan smiled, delight rising in her like water from a geyser. "No. In fact, I'm in a serious relationship. He's coming to the wedding."

"Then I look forward to meeting him."

"Good. And I look forward to you meeting him as well."

Rafe quirked a brow. "Okay."

"It's just that Geoff is everything I've ever wanted. He's loyal, devoted and will do anything for me." A little worried she'd made Geoff sound like a dog, she made a mental note to pull back on the praise. "He also wants to start a family right away."

"I'm happy for you."

"Thanks."

"Are you planning on a big wedding?"

"Um, well, I haven't set a date. It's imminent, though."

"If he's a smart man he won't let you get away."

She blinked, a little stunned by the compliment. In the way of conversation, she had nothing that felt safe enough to bring up, so she reached.

"So, do you have a date to the wedding?"

He nodded, tipping back on his heels. "Susan is my date."

"I've heard a lot about her."

"She's smart and funny, too. You'll love her."

"I'm sure I will."

Gosh, they were being so civil to each other. Jordan had wanted to throw a goblet of champagne in his face, but she'd done a fair job of containing her anger. Besides, she'd never ruin this moment for Ava.

Speaking of Ava, all eyes turned when she sashayed out of the dressing room and stepped on the pedestal in the most incredible wedding dress Jordan had ever laid eyes on. The satin dress had a fitted bodice that flared out past her thighs in a mermaid-style silhouette. Ava had the perfect figure for it. A sweetheart collar completed the look, giving her a positively royal appearance.

"Oh, Ava!" Stacy covered her mouth.

Valerie wiped away tears. "You look like Princess Grace of Monaco. Or some other princess."

"Doesn't she?" Dr. Long went behind Ava, inspecting the short and elegant flared train.

"Que bonita!" said Lucia as she joined Dr. Long.

"Your brother is one lucky guy," Rafe remarked.

"If you'll excuse me, I have to get to work."

And with that, Jordan turned away from Rafe and went back to her happy place.

Chapter Three

Jordan's black hair was no longer long, wavy and wild: she wore it shorter, to her neck, cut in sharp, clean angles. Her round caramel eyes were hooded and unreadable to him. Once, before he'd ruined it all, everything he'd ever wanted was reflected in her gaze. Love. Warmth. A future.

In addition to her appearance, it seemed everything about Jordan had changed, too. A sharpness in her gaze and in her very posture threw him, but what did he expect? Over four years might as well be four decades for all the changes they'd both been through.

During his career in Special Forces, Rafe had been a tactical explosives expert. He'd worn his suit of Kevlar, plating and foam. Still no guarantee he'd survive the blast.

This moment reminded him of that.

"More?" A store clerk held the champagne bottle in front of Rafe. "I'm Becca, nice to meet you."

"Rafe." He held out his flute of orange juice mixed with a splash of champagne. "Why not. I seem to be the only one indulging."

"I would join you, but I'm working."

Jordan flitted around the shop, taking notes in a leather book, laughing and joking with the bridesmaids. However, she seemed extremely concerned about the strapless dresses, which Rafe thought were fine.

Ava's mother and someone named Lucia now clucked and fussed over Ava's wedding veil.

"It should really be a tiara," her mother said. "Don't you think, Lucia?"

"Ah, yes. What about a tiara? I agree with your *mami.*"

For the next few minutes everyone busied themselves with tiara versus veil, finally winding up on tiara territory. By then, Rafe regretted this outing, which had essentially worked out to be an exercise in mental self-flagellation.

This was his fault, after all. He'd married Liz despite all his plans with Jordan, or the fact they'd loved each other for what felt like forever. In his heart he knew Jordan would survive. She had a large family and plenty of support.

"Thank you, I will have some." Lucia held out a flute to the clerk. "We have at last decided on the tiara."

"Congratulations," Rafe muttered.

"This must all seem very boring, you poor man." Lucia's heavy accent reminded Rafe of his late grandmother, who'd immigrated to California from Portugal decades ago.

He stood and held out his hand. "Rafe Reyes."

"Lucia Perez. Nice to meet you. Which one of these beauties is your woman?" She gestured toward the ladies gathered around Ava.

"No one," he said, mildly aware the clerk appeared to be eavesdropping on their conversation. "I brought Cole's wife, Valerie. She's the pregnant one."

"Ay, si. Buena suerte con los hijos." She waved a hand. "She's having a boy. That's what I think."

Rafe managed a smile. "And how do you know the bride?"

"I raised Ava," she said, somewhat triumphantly. "I was her nanny for eighteen years of her life. She's like my own daughter."

"Max and I grew up together, and to tell the truth, I've never seen him this happy."

"Oh, yes, *mijita* has a way of doing that to people. She brings the happy everywhere she goes. My nickname for her was 'Felicia,' which means 'happy girl' in Spanish." She sent him a significant look. "And forgive me, but it looks like you need a little *felicidad*."

"It shows?"

"I wouldn't expect many men excited to be here, but you look especially disgusted."

"Sorry," Rafe said. "I'm disgusted with *myself*, and nothing, or no one else."

"Oh no. That will not do. You're far too young to be disgusted with yourself." Lucia shook a finger.

Rafe chuckled. "If you say so."

"Lucia. We need you." Ava's mother waved Lucia over.

"You will join us for lunch. I will not hear the word no." Lucia bustled away to join the others.

This time the fascination seemed to be with the long skirt of the dress. The stylist gathered it in her hands, and then so did Dr. Long. Even Jordan seemed fascinated. He didn't understand, but what the hell did he know?

He and Liz hadn't had a wedding reception or party. They'd gotten it all over quickly, gone to the justice of the peace. Liz, a helo pilot, wasn't the type for pomp and circumstance, either. They were two soldiers doing the best they could.

"I get off work at five." Becca smiled and handed Rafe a card.

He took it before he knew what he'd accepted. Staring at the card, he realized he'd just been hit on for what felt like the first time in years. Apparently "dad" wasn't stamped across his forehead.

Good to know.

Leave it to Lucia to invite Rafe for lunch at the Salty Dog. Their group had to split into two separate booths, and Dr. Long, Lucia and Ava sat in one booth. Jordan wanted to be with them, but she'd made the mistake of taking a seat before she realized the division. And before she could stop him, Rafe took a seat next to her, Valerie and Stacy across from them. His long muscular thigh next to hers was like a firebrand. Jordan kept turning her knees in the opposite direction, avoiding contact, because any brush of him against her leg gave tingles she didn't want to have.

Instead of discussing the wedding, which they were likely doing at the other table, Jordan listened to nothing but talk of babies and children. She had nothing to contribute. Stacy asked about Valerie's latest ultrasound. After that subject had been exhausted, Stacy brought up her baby girl's teething.

"Try freezing a baby towel and letting her chew on that," Rafe offered.

"At this point we'll try anything."

"I love that you have all these tips," Valerie said. "Trial by fire."

"If not for Adam…I don't know what I'd do. He gets up during the night with Tennessee. Now that I've weaned her, we're trying to get her to stay in her crib all night." Stacy sighed.

Jordan glanced briefly at Rafe to find him studying her once more. At the wedding shop, he'd been flirting with the salesclerk. Or she with him. Either way. None of her concern.

All four of them ate, the conversation light. But with Rafe in the same room, next to her, nothing could be casual and easygoing enough for Jordan. She picked at her salad, appetite gone.

Stacy suddenly grabbed her cell phone and purse. "Almost forgot, I have to get home. Adam has a thing."

"Oh, would you drop me off later?" Valerie asked Stacy. "Rafe gave me a ride, and he's not done eating." She turned to Rafe. "You go ahead and finish, and Stacy will drive me home. This way I'll get to see Tennessee."

They were about to open their wallets, but Rafe held up a hand. "My treat."

"Really, our husbands are the owners. You don't have to—" Valerie said.

"Please, let me. It's the least I can do. You're letting me and Susan stay in your beautiful home."

"We'll see you at the wedding rehearsal if I don't catch you before then," Stacy said with a quick wave.

They were off a moment later, saying their hasty goodbyes to Ava in the other booth.

"Well, I should go, too." Jordan picked up her purse. But Rafe didn't move. She waited a beat. And waited another. "Rafe?"

"Yeah?" He studied her from underneath long lashes, eyes slightly amused.

"Uh, move?"

"Not yet." He shifted his body, turning toward her. "Talk to me. Are we going to be awkward around each other the entire time?"

She swallowed thickly. "No, Rafe, we're going to get along for the sake of Max."

"It doesn't feel that way."

"Well. Maybe you're asking too much. Did that occur to you?"

He reached for her hand and damn if she didn't feel warmth tug at her soul. "Please, *cielito*. I never meant to hurt you."

She pulled her hand back. "You can't help who you love, can you?"

"You have a big family and you're strong. Capable. Always were."

"I *am*, which is a good thing because I always came last with you."

He flinched like she'd slapped him. "That's not true."

"Really?"

She gave him a minute to reconsider and remember how many missions he'd been on and how many times he'd been deployed while she waited for him. And waited.

"You were everything."

"Until I wasn't." Jordan's cell pinged—thank you, Jesus. Caller ID said it was Geoff. She held up her cell. "I have to answer this. It's the man I love."

"Go ahead." He made a motion for her to answer. "I can wait."

"I would like very much for you to let me out of this booth right now, please."

He gave her a slow smile, then slid out of the booth.

"Thank you." Jordan strode outside.

She crossed the boardwalk and headed to the seawall. The early spring day was already heating up. Her hair was going to cut loose any minute and she'd probably resemble a Latina Orphan Annie. At times like these she wished she'd kept her hair long. This blowout wasn't going to outlast the humid Southwest weather.

"Hey, I have bad news," Geoff said.

"What's happened now?"

"Looks like I'm going to be tied up with this trial until after the wedding. So sorry, sweetheart. I'll make it up to you."

"You have *got* to be kidding me! Can't you tell the boss you've already made plans? You have plane tickets. This is ridiculous. They don't own you."

"Of course, they don't. You own me." He chuckled. "But if I want to make partner in the next couple of years like we planned, I've got to become indispensable to them."

How about becoming indispensable to me?

It did not escape Jordan that she'd only loved two men in her life and both of them had put their career before her. But she couldn't argue with Geoff's reasoning. They were two of a kind—a goal-oriented, forward-moving couple who had a strategic plan. He wasn't off fighting a war in another country, dismantling bombs, risking his life at every turn. Geoff was doing important work, too, representing people who'd been wronged. Making partner would be everything he'd worked for. Everything she'd supported. Someday, this would be worth their struggle.

"Well... I'm going to be so busy I wouldn't have had much time for you anyway."

"Thank you. I *really* don't deserve you."

"No, you don't."

"When you get home, we'll take a weekend getaway, just the two of us. Maybe to Napa Valley."

"That sounds wonderful."

After hanging up, Jordan stood by the seawall for a few minutes, letting the sun rays bathe her skin, listening to the sound of the crashing waves. The seagulls foraged for tourists' leftovers. At the other end of the boardwalk were carnival rides and games. Families were out in force, putting up umbrellas, setting out blankets to spend the day.

The weekend getaway to wine country sounded great but probably wouldn't happen. Geoff would have to work, or she would, since spring and summer events were one of her busiest times.

Sometimes, when she stood in front of the gaping and vast ocean, she questioned the future, and when all these years of hard work would pay off. Because at the moment, the answer seemed to be *never*.

"Everything okay?"

Rafe stood behind her, hands stuck in the pockets of his jeans, looking completely unconcerned with the day's humidity. His dark wavy hair sat on his head where it was supposed to and didn't look in any danger of putting somebody's eye out.

"It's all fine. But you won't be meeting Geoff.

He got tied up in pretrial motions and will miss the wedding."

"Damn, I'm sorry."

She stuck her cell in her purse. "No big deal. I would have been too busy to pay him much attention."

"So, what happens now?"

"What happens *now*? I have a wedding to put on. Thousands of tiny details. The wedding rehearsal is next week."

"I'll be there." He grinned and tipped back on his heels. "Let me know if I can do anything to help you out."

"Tell me how you manage to look so cool in this weather?" She fanned herself with a piece of paper and wiped away a trickle of sweat from her neck. He, however, didn't seem to be breaking a sweat.

"Ah, I'm used to it by now."

"Right. Well, my hair is used to California weather. I'm afraid it's going to bust loose any minute and hurt somebody." She smoothed back a stray curl.

Her blowout days were numbered. She should have had her stylist use the permanent chemical solution.

"I always loved your hair. Loved it long, too." He made a sweeping motion with his hands. "How long has it been flat like that?"

"About three years. Why?"

Self-conscious, she smoothed her hair down. And

it wasn't *flat*, but straight. Stylish. Sleek and sophisticated. *Expensive.*

"Just curious."

Panic hit and she dug through her purse. "Did you get stuck with the entire bill for our table? I meant to pay for my portion."

He held up his palm in the universal stop sign. "We're good. Let me treat you. It's the least I can do."

"It's the least you can do?" she parroted the remark, sounding snarky because God knew he could and should do better than picking up her lunch tab.

"I can do a lot more, but that's going to be entirely up to you." His voice sounded as smooth and rich as espresso.

All manner of saucy thoughts raced through her feverish brain. Probably because she and Rafe had always spent more time under the sheets than on top of them.

"Like…what, exactly?"

"I'll be your assistant if you need one." He lifted a shoulder. "Order me around. You know you'll feel better."

"This will come as a shock, but I don't need you." She meant the remark to be cutting but he didn't seem even slightly fazed.

"Well, I'm here if you change your mind."

"Daddy! Daddy!" A blonde whirlwind appeared at Rafe's side in a flash, Sub and Cole right behind her.

Chapter Four

Susan Kelly was adorable, with bright blue eyes and a beamish smile. Naturally, she didn't look anything like Rafe. Instead, she greatly favored Liz. Ultimately, the decision to marry Liz had been Rafe's, and he'd been the one to betray Jordan. But for a long while, Jordan had deeply resented Liz, too. She'd fallen in love with her late husband's friend and hadn't cared whom she hurt in the process.

"Hey, Shortie." Rafe bent to pick the little girl up. "I want you to meet someone very special. This is my friend Jordan Del Toro. Jordan and her brother Max were my best friends growing up."

"Hi!" She waved with a huge smile.

"Hi, Susan." Jordan couldn't help but smile back. "I've heard a lot about you."

"Sorry, guys," Cole said. "There's a problem in the kitchen and with Max in a meeting and Adam with the baby, I had to run over. But we had a great time making sandcastles. We'll do it again soon, next time with Valerie."

"You just missed her." Rafe put Susan down. "Did you behave for Cole?"

"She did." Cole tousled her hair, then waved as he walked inside the bar, Sub following.

"Daddy, I want a dog," Susan said. "Just like Sub."

Rafe smirked. "I'll see what I can do."

"Do you have any pets at home?" Jordan asked, making casual conversation.

This little girl might have changed the trajectory of Jordan's life, but Susan had no choice in the matter. She was a complete innocent in their dysfunctional mess.

"I have a cat at my mommy's house. His name is Fatso." She giggled. "Because he's fat and lays around all day."

"And you have fish in my apartment," Rafe said. "An aquarium full of them."

"Fish are dumb. I want a dog."

Which, Jordan had to assume, might be difficult in an apartment.

Rafe reached for his daughter's hand. "How about some cotton candy instead as a consolation prize?"

"Yes!" At the promise of sugar, she seemed to forget the dog. "And I want to go on a ride. But not the scary ones."

"No, of course not."

Jordan prepared to say goodbye when Susan grabbed her hand. "Okay, let's go!"

"Me? Oh no, I'm… I was…"

"Do you like cotton candy, yes or no?" Susan tugged, completely clueless that Jordan might have other plans.

Jordan followed along, trying to figure out a way to get out of this. She'd been around enough of her nieces and nephews to understand that young kids didn't know they weren't the center of the galaxy. But surely Rafe understood. She caught his eye and urged him to get her out of this, but he didn't read her signals.

"She likes sweet and salty kettle corn and pretends she doesn't like cotton candy." Rafe winked. "But she does."

The memory on this man unnerved her. But he'd been her first love, her first…everything. It could be said once he'd understood her better than anyone else other than family. He knew how important it was for the Del Toros to rise above their humble beginnings picking in the strawberry fields of Watsonville. Particularly for Jordan and Max, who were the oldest, born only eighteen months apart. Like her big brother, Jordan had worked hard to make a better life. Unlike Max, Jordan had too often let emotions rule her.

However, if Rafe remembered so much about her, why didn't he understand that she couldn't go with him and Susan to a *carnival*? She had things to do, people to call, flower deliveries to confirm and a yoga class to book. Lately, she'd been letting that last one go. Not wise under these stressful conditions. She pulled her planner out and stopped to make a note to look into local yoga classes.

A moment later, Rafe thrust in her hands a large bag of kettle popcorn, which she nearly dropped. "You're welcome, Zippy."

See, it wasn't fair to call her by the childhood nickname. "I can't eat this."

"Why?" This was from Susan, an honest question from an inquisitive four-year-old.

Because it has a bazillion calories? She didn't want to give the girl the idea that body size mattered, and a woman should be preoccupied with calorie counting. But...well... Rafe was studying her, his brow quirked.

"It's not...healthy for me," Jordan explained.

"But why?"

"It has a lot of sugar in it, which contributes to obesity."

"But why?"

"Our bodies aren't meant to process this much sugar."

"But why?"

Dear Lord, would she ever stop? Seriously, how long could she keep this up? "Because that's the way our bodies are designed."

"But why?"

"Look! It's the merry-go-round!" Jordan pointed, going for distraction as a means to end The Inquisition.

"I want to ride the horsie." Susan pointed and ran ahead.

"Hey! Why didn't you *save* me from that interrogation?" Jordan hissed.

Rafe picked up his pace. "It was fun. And impressive. For what it's worth, you lasted longer than I do."

Rafe took Jordan's hand and a jolt of awareness coursed through her. "C'mon, I could use the help. You don't mind, do you?"

"Well, I…"

But father was just as good as daughter at listening. He tugged her along through the families crowding the boardwalk, following Susan, a streak of lightning ahead of them. This didn't seem safe. Jordan considered taking Rafe to task for letting his daughter run ahead in the midst of complete strangers. What if someone abducted her? She could picture Rafe easily catching up to whoever would be foolish enough to grab his daughter. But on the other hand, he was beginning to seem a lot less tense than she remembered him.

The Rafe she'd known had a singular purpose in life: join the service, get his education, then rise in rank. He let nothing or no *one* derail his plans. Present company included. He had planned to be career military but obviously Susan had changed his priorities. Susan and *Liz*. He seemed so casual and relaxed now. He was no longer the tightly wound, buttoned-up military man who would come home from missions and speak to her in one-word sentences for weeks.

They'd reached the carousel where Susan had the presence of mind to stop and wait for them. Rafe finally released Jordan's hand.

"C'mon," Susan said, and grabbed Rafe's hand on one side and Jordan's on the other.

"What? I'm not…"

Dressed for this, *or* ready for this.

"Don't be afraid," Susan said, squeezing Jordan's hand. "I'm here. I won't let anything happen to you."

The words sounded so stunningly adult that for a moment Jordan could only stare at the little girl. Because she heard Rafe's words echoed, carried through the years, repeated now by this precious little girl. *Don't be afraid. I'm here.*

Her eyes flitted to Rafe, who studied her with soulful dark eyes. His gaze had been famous for squeezing all manner of emotions from Jordan, usually followed by actions, like removing all of her clothes.

"I think Jordan has things to do right now," he said softly.

"No, she doesn't. She *wants* to go. Right?" Hopeful eyes turned to Jordan, searching her with such innocence that something inside stirred.

"I'll go with you." Jordan held up her finger. "But just one ride, and then I have to go plan a wedding."

Rafe helped Susan hop up on the platform, then held his hand out for Jordan. Susan skipped ahead of the other children, causing Jordan to bob and weave in order to keep up.

Susan eventually chose a beautiful white horse. The kind Prince Charming would ride. "This one!"

Rafe plopped her on it and cinched in the belt. He took her chin and met her eyes. "You okay?"

"Yes, Daddy. I'm going to be okay."

Rafe wound up on one side of the horse, Jordan on the other, holding on to the pole as the carousel went slowly around. The music playing was familiar, taking her back to when she was seventeen. She and Rafe had been at the State Fair when the Ferris wheel had gotten stuck. They were stranded near the top, and she'd used the extra time for a heavy make-out session with Rafe. Until Max began throwing kernels of popcorn at them from where he sat above them with his flavor-of-the-month girlfriend.

Jordan's gaze went back to Rafe, and he sent her a slow smile. She didn't smile back but looked away, finding Susan, eyes shut, a little smile on her lips. Curious. Part of the fun was watching everything go around in a spinning pattern, waving at people on the sidelines. Then again, Susan had her two people next to her with no one in particular to wave to.

The ride ended and Rafe helped her off the horse. "You did really good, honey."

"See? I wasn't even afraid." On the base of the

carousel, Susan grabbed on to Jordan's waist and squeezed. "I wasn't afraid."

Shocked at the sudden rush of affection, Jordan patted the little girl's head. She caught Rafe watching, a look of tenderness softening his usually sharp and angular features.

"That's...that's good," Jordan said. "It's good to be brave."

Without letting go, Susan turned her face up and offered a sweet, dimpled smile that cracked open Jordan's tightly controlled heart.

Chapter Five

"Tomorrow morning, can I look through the teta-scope again?" Susan asked.

"Telescope." Rafe tucked the covers around her. "Yes, you may."

Since arriving, she'd been fascinated with the old-fashioned telescope on the upper deck of the converted lighthouse. On a clear day, one could almost see Galveston and cruise ships in the distance leaving port. Susan, for her part, saw mermaids.

Different strokes.

Tonight, it had taken four stories, his standard homespun fairy tale, three different trips for water and then resulting need for the bathroom, before her eyelids showed the slightest inclination to droop. It was cruel the way kids could outlast their parents.

When he had Susan every other weekend for visitation, he was often ready to pass out long before her.

"I had fun with your friend," Susan said, finally yawning.

"Jordan."

"She's pretty."

"Yeah, I know. She is." He ruffled her hair and brushed his eyelashes across her cheek for standard nighttime butterfly kisses.

Susan giggled and turned her cheek. "But she's *not* as pretty as Mommy. And she's kind of like Mrs. Leah."

Rafe struggled to decipher how Jordan reminded Susan of her fiftysomething-year-old preschool teacher. The woman reminded *him* far too much of the horrible school administrator from the Harry Potter books.

"How's she like Mrs. Leah?"

"You know, like Mommy says. Mrs. Leah has the stick up her butt." She giggled. "That's funny."

Rafe winced. "Okay, don't say that again. About Jordan *or* Mrs. Leah."

"But why? Is it a bad word?"

"It's not *nice*. Remember what I said?"

She scrunched up her nose. "You say a lot of things."

"In a world in which you can be anything, be *kind*." He moved to the bedroom door and stood in the archway. "Good night, honey."

"Good night, Daddy."

As he slowly shut the door, he heard Susan yell, "Don't close it all the way!"

"How's that?" he asked, leaving it ajar a good twelve inches.

"Okay."

"I'm not far. Don't be afraid. I'm here with you."

Another prick of guilt sliced through him. Susan had regressed in the six months since he and Liz had officially divorced. Suddenly, his happy-go-lucky daughter was fearful of the dark, and occasionally afraid to sleep alone. She threw tantrums such as he hadn't seen since she was two. Finally, she'd come to an end with the fits. Fingers crossed it would remain this way.

Were he being honest with himself, she'd been regressing since she'd had enough awareness to realize that Mommy and Daddy didn't kiss and hug the way other parents did.

He worried sometimes she might have overheard his tense arguments with Liz, late at night after they were certain she'd gone to sleep. Liz would drink a little too much and start hurling accusations:

"You don't love me, and you never did."

Maybe not, but he'd tried. He'd been a faithful and loyal husband. But in the end, he was a far better father. Eventually, Liz had wanted more from him. Even the crusty former helo pilot wanted more love, more joy. Passion. And he believed she deserved it. A year and a half ago, when she'd found someone who would give her that, Rafe was mainly worried how their divorce would affect Susan.

He'd already experienced that hard-to-find, knock-you-on-your-ass love that slammed into a person's heart with the force of a sonic bomb. Every once in a while paranoia struck, and he feared he would have to pay dearly for turning his back on a once-in-a-lifetime kind of love.

Jordan was as beautiful as he remembered, and now he had the additional piercing knowledge that nothing had changed with his heart or mind when it came to her. He still felt that undeniable pull of attraction toward her, still raw and fresh and new. But now she was with another man. *Exactly* what Rafe deserved. It was the universal law of reciprocity and he couldn't be surprised. He would now get to watch her with someone else and pretend none of it mattered.

But they'd been friends first, and he pledged he'd behave and support her in every way.

Because that's what I do. Yeah, he was such a damn good guy that he couldn't manage to salvage his own marriage for the sake of his daughter. He listened briefly in the hallway for the soft even sounds of Susan sleeping and came downstairs to join Valerie and Cole. They were sitting on the L-shaped couch, Sub at their feet like a rug.

"Have I thanked you for putting up with me and my daughter?"

"About once a day. She's adorable." Valerie reached

to tousle her husband's hair. "And Cole needs the practice."

As a third grade teacher, Valerie was way ahead of her husband when it came to children.

"You don't have to lie. I know she's a handful."

"Well…" Cole began. "She does ask *a lot* of questions. She must have asked me 'why' a hundred times."

"Aw, he's just not used to children."

"Guess not. I expect the questioning to end at some point," Cole said, shaking his head.

Rafe laughed, remembering Jordan's trial by fire. She'd handled the situation far better than he would have expected. Still, pink had colored her cheeks in frustration, and he'd had to bite back a laugh.

"That's pretty typical behavior for kids her age, but she's also been struggling since Liz and I separated."

"That's common," Valerie said. "We see it all the time at school. The sad thing is, even when children live in the most difficult of situations, they want their parents to stay together."

"Well, that's never going to happen."

"You sure?" Cole said.

"The divorce is final and neither one of us is looking back."

"She'll be okay, Rafe." Valerie's tone was gentle, reassuring. "I promise you. Kids are resilient and as long as you love her, and I know you do, she's going to be fine."

Later, after Cole and Valerie had gone to bed for the night, Rafe took a walk outside along the beach. The moon glinted off the shore, the night clear and bright. Though Rafe appreciated Valerie's kind words, and hoped they were true, he couldn't help but feel like a failure.

He'd once read that the best thing a father could ever do for his child was love their mother.

And he'd failed, God knew he had, but he just hadn't been able to love Liz the way she deserved.

Love wasn't enough, either, because he'd loved Jordan with everything he had but failed her too. She'd spent years waiting for him between deployments, putting up with him when he had a difficult time readjusting to civilian life. They'd been a team, and she was ready to sign on as a military wife. To support him in every way. Somewhere along the line she'd lost faith in him.

And the memory of that loss was still a solid punch to the gut.

"This is unacceptable," Jordan said. "These are *not* the wedding favors we ordered."

For the only daughter of two Dallas physicians, no expense had been spared. These favors were beautifully designed glass Tiffany jewelry boxes from a high-end store in Dallas, sent to an artist who had decorated them with the engraved names of the bride and groom, ribbons affixed with a pearl-like flower on top.

It was now T-minus ten days before wedding day and the favors had violet ribbons, not *blue* as she'd specifically ordered.

"What do you mean?" said the clerk, lowering her gaze. "The artist usually does great work."

"They were supposed to be *blue*, not violet. See?" Jordan pointed to the violet ribbon on top. "Blue and silver is the color scheme, not violet and silver."

"Oh, I see." Over lowered spectacles, the clerk inspected the ribbon. "Close enough?"

"No."

She sighed. "I'll send it back to the designer and we'll get it fixed."

"How long?" Jordan's heart slammed against her rib cage, her palms growing sweaty.

"A couple of weeks?"

"I don't *have* a couple of weeks."

"Well, I guess then maybe you should have ordered a bit sooner to avoid any delays like this."

Jordan squashed the murderous thoughts those words brought about. If only people paid attention to detail the way *she* did, there would be no need to anticipate errors. To *plan* for mistakes. But yes, Jordan *should* have ordered from her preferred vendor in California and brought them to Texas in her own suitcases. She'd attempted to convince her brother to have their wedding in California, and Ava was game. But Ava's family had been insistent. They were already making a *sacrifice* by having the nuptials in

Charming, and not Dallas, among all their hoity-toity high-society friends.

"Do you have any *blue* ribbon?" Jordan asked through clenched teeth. "And also, I'll need a glue gun."

Thirty minutes later, she had several boxes of wedding favors—five hundred to be exact—laid on her hotel room bed.

Okay. Deep breaths.

It was not like she hadn't done this kind of thing before. She'd helped with her brother Lou's wedding favors a few years ago. But she'd never worked with Tiffany designer boxes, ribbon and a hot glue gun. She should ask for help, but from whom? Sherry, her assistant, was in California holding down the fort, her family wouldn't arrive for several more days and Geoff didn't give a damn. He was in "trial prep" when the world stopped rotating.

She briefly wondered if the clerk was right and no one else would notice violet versus blue. But no. Only a color-blind person wouldn't notice, and she was certain Dr. Long, the mother, and the other esteemed Dr. Long, who were spending a small fortune for this wedding, would *notice*.

She rubbed her hands together. "Okay. Who needs to sleep, anyway? It's highly overrated."

She changed into the yoga pants and T-shirt she lived in when no one was watching, and began the brutally slow process. Within an hour, she had two boxes done. They looked perfect if she did say so herself. Silver and *blue*.

Given two boxes per hour, she should be done in approximately…two-hundred and forty-nine hours. So, basically, ten days. If she didn't sleep. Well, she'd simply have to step up production. She'd get the hang of it after a few more.

Two hours later, even she was beginning to appreciate the violet ribbons.

Her cell rang and she reached for it, needing the break from this tedium. "Hey, Max. Why didn't you *tell* me Rafe divorced Liz?"

There was a pause. "You told me to never say his name out loud again."

"Well, I didn't mean it, did I?"

"Is that why you walked out of the room every time I even casually said his name? I didn't think it was my job to keep you up to date on Rafe's life. If you wanted to know, you could have asked. Or even talked to the man himself."

"Fine. Your point is made. What can I do for you?"

"I need you to talk to Ava." The sounds of loud chatting and silverware clinking in the background meant Max was at the restaurant.

"What's wrong?"

"She's upset."

"Um, care to elaborate?"

"I would, but I already forgot what this is about. We're slammed tonight. It has something to do with a song, or…a color."

"Gosh, Max, *you're* a big help."

"All I know is she's upset. She's almost crying, and I can't take that. I need you to *fix* it."

"Me?"

Apparently, she'd become so adept at her work people thought she could fix everything. From the corner of her eye, she caught sight of the favors strewn all over her bed and didn't have to wonder for long where people came up with this idea.

"Yes, *you*. You're the wedding planner, aren't you?"

She was dealing with her older brother, former navy SEAL and now successful businessman and restaurateur.

He expected a lot from the people he loved.

"Wedding planner extraordinaire, at your service. And beck and call. And…whatever. I don't need sleep."

"Great, I knew I could count on you."

Chapter Six

Jordan met Ava at the Salty Dog, finding her seated on a stool at the bar watching Max. He must be doing his occasional "step in where needed" and bartending tonight.

Ava met Jordan with a warm hug. "Thank you for coming."

"Of course, of course. Now, how can I help?" Jordan led them to an empty booth and waved for Ava to sit. "Max said you're upset. I never like to see one of my brides upset. There's no reason for that. And you're obviously very special to me, so whatever it is, I'm here to fix it."

While Jordan *couldn't* fix a reluctant bride or groom, this was at least one matter she would not need to worry about.

"Max said you would help. He says you're the kind of person everyone comes to with their problems."

A ripple of warm pride pulsed through her. "Oh, I don't know about that."

Still, it was good to hear that her older brother had such faith in her. Once, it hadn't been that way at all. She'd been a floundering young adult, unsure what to do with the rest of her life. Education was the answer, but she had no idea what to study, and wouldn't waste money until she found out first. Meanwhile, Max and Rafe had enlisted straight out of high school and received their education via the United States Government. She'd stood on the sidelines and watched in admiration as they achieved every goal they set out to make.

"See, I'm kind of upset." And given by Ava's trembling lower lip, there was no "kind of" about it.

"What is it? Whatever it is, we can take care of this."

Given time.

Jordan whipped out her book and noted how many days left until the wedding day. She hoped this problem could be resolved easily, because adding another chore meant calling in extra help. Or somehow figuring out how to clone herself.

"Well…it's… See, my father loves jazz."

"Uh-huh."

A song. At least Max was in the ballpark. Jordan opened up her planner to the pages for "Ava and Max's wedding."

"And he hired a string quartet to play jazz." Ava wrung her hands together. "At *my* reception."

Okay, why did Jordan not know about this? This was vital information. Vital. She flipped through her book maniacally. Nothing. People couldn't dance to jazz music. Jesus! Was it hot in here?

"You don't like jazz."

"I *hate* jazz." Ava now drummed her fingers on the table. "Hate. It."

"But w-what happened to the DJ? I have the name written down *right here*." Jordan tapped on the page in her planner. If it was written in her book, it was solid law.

"Oh, I forgot to tell you. My father cancelled the DJ."

Forgot…forgot to *tell* her? Jordan scrawled a note about jazz quartets and DJs.

"Okay, so we need to find another option. I'll make a call and try to use my influence to get the DJ back." She clasped her hands together. "If we're lucky. Have you talked to your father about this?"

"Did I mention my father loves jazz music?"

"Ava, this is *your* wedding."

"Yes, but my father finally retired and he's looking for things to do. My mother said he wants to be involved in my wedding. And I feel bad. He *really* loves jazz."

"I appreciate that, but we can find other ways for him to contribute."

No one can dance to jazz!

"He's paying for the wedding. All of it. Max wanted to but my father insisted. I'm his only daughter. So that's why we're having this huge reception with my mother's favorite French cuisine caterer and an ice sculpture in the shape of two doves." Ava chewed on her lower lip.

Ah, yes, the *ice sculpture*. Jordan flipped through her planner and found the contact information. All top-tier weddings had one. It had been one less thing for her to worry about. Yes, this was a sophisticated wedding, making her once again rest assured the wedding favors had to be *just right*. Her instincts were still top-notch.

Jordan patted Ava's hand. "Leave it all to me. *I'll* talk to your father and we'll find another way for him to feel significant on your special day."

"Oh my gosh, you would do that for me?" Ava's face brightened.

"Hello?" She held her palms out to the side. "Ta-da! Wedding planner extraordinaire here."

"Thank you, thank you, thank you!" Ava came around to Jordan's side of the bench and threw her arms around her. "I'm going to go tell Max this is fixed. He would talk to my father, but I think it will be better coming from you."

No doubt. She could only imagine how her alpha, overprotective brother would stride in like a bull in a china shop and *tell* Ava's father the string quartet was out. Whatever Ava wanted—song, color, he had no clue—but that was in.

Jordan would find a way to make it Ava's father's idea. Yes, she had a gift. Jordan smiled and watched Ava go behind the bar. Max dropped everything he was doing and enveloped Ava in a hug so tender and warm that for a moment Jordan's heart ached.

Geoff *never* hugged Jordan. He seemed to have two settings when it came to her: all business and sexy times. So much could be said for the comfort of a good hug, one which reached all the way into your heart. She'd always wanted to be at the center of a man's life, just like her *mami* was for her *papi*. It wasn't too much to ask.

The doors to the Salty Dog suddenly opened, and Jordan looked up to find Rafe holding the door for a woman. Jordan recognized the woman, too—the bridal clerk from the dress fittings. No surprise, Rafe already had a date. They were seated on the restaurant side of the bar—thank you, God—and Jordan was on the other side closer to the bar. Good. She didn't want to meet Rafe's date, when she couldn't even get Geoff, her boyfriend of two *years*, to come to her brother's wedding with her.

Okay, this wasn't a competition. But unfortunately, ever since the day Rafe had dropped her for Liz, Jordan often wondered why she hadn't been *enough*. Liz was also military, a pilot, and very accomplished in her own career. At the time, Jordan had still been struggling to find her way. She should be well over this kind of thing by now, this type of comparison, but the display had wrenched her right back to the not-so-distant past.

Waving quickly in Max and Ava's direction, Jordan slipped out of the restaurant before Rafe could notice.

Rafe wasn't sure he'd done the right thing, but in an apparently temporary bout of amnesia, he'd gone ahead and called Becca. He'd forgotten that the date thing hadn't worked out too well last time and this time probably wouldn't be any different. But Valerie and Cole were home relaxing and watching Tennessee Rose anyway, so they'd urged Rafe to get out for a little "me time." Susan was absolutely delighted by baby Tennessee.

He would prefer spending his "me time" with Jordan, but that would not accomplish the goal of getting him out into the world to possibly meet someone new. Someone with whom he could have a future and build a life. Liz had already moved on, and on not too fine a point, so had Jordan. But no one sparked anything in him and hadn't for years. He was a red-blooded male and given that he hadn't had sex in almost two years, and the last woman had been Liz, he was definitely chomping at the bit.

So, he was supposed to put himself through this process which felt as comfortable as diffusing a bomb some days.

This is what happens when you never learned how to date.

Except for their few brief breakups, Rafe hadn't ever *dated* anyone but Jordan. And she'd been less of a date than a teenage sweetheart. Liz had become his wife without a single date. The realization hit him that he no longer had any idea how to do this.

"I can't tell you how much I admire single dads and all you do," Becca said.

Some of Susan's caregivers thought he was over-involved. Friends couldn't understand why he'd stepped in to raise another man's child.

But after Lieutenant Travis Kelly's death, Liz and Susan had no one but him. Rafe would have stepped in front of a moving freight train for Kelly. Marrying his widow and raising their daughter was a sacrifice he'd made for the man who'd once saved Rafe's life. Without a husband, Liz would have likely never been deployed again. After marrying Rafe, she was able to complete two more deployments while Rafe retired from Special Forces to care for Susan. In a way, Rafe had been a single dad all along.

"So, you're from California?" Becca asked after they'd placed their orders. "I've been to California."

"From Watsonville. Are you familiar with it?"

She wrinkled her nose. "Is that near San Francisco?"

Ah, yes. To people not from California, there were two cities in the entire state: San Francisco and Los Angeles.

"It's closer to Santa Cruz."

"Oh, yes. I've heard of it. A big surfing community, right?"

"Right."

Rafe's phone buzzed in his pocket. He'd told himself he wouldn't look, but what if it was something important? Susan was hundreds of miles from home and if anything went wrong, Liz would castrate him. At the least, she'd stop allowing him visitation out of the kindness of her heart. Rafe had no parental rights.

Thoughts like these sometimes made it difficult to breathe.

"Excuse me for a second," he said, noting the call was from Cole's cell. He held up a finger to Becca and spoke into the phone. "Hey. What's up?"

"Daddy?" came Susan's voice.

"Honey, you're supposed to call me only if it's an emergency."

"It *is* an emergency. I can't find my wand. I want to turn Tennessee from a pumpkin into a princess and I can't find my magic wand."

While Rafe loved this age of make-believe Susan had become firmly entrenched in, he would be the first to admit it could be a bit exhausting.

"Did you look in my suitcase?"

"I can't find it. You better come here and help me look."

"I'm going to be home soon. We talked about this."

"Oh, I'm sorry, Rafe," came Valerie's voice. "She somehow got a hold of Cole's phone. I'm not sure how she figured out the password. But everything's fine now. Say goodbye to your daddy. He'll be home lickety-split."

"Bye, Daddy," Susan said.

His daughter was as bright as they came. After all, she was the biological daughter of a brilliant tactical explosives expert. By the time she was three, she'd figured out the password for his phone.

Rafe hung up, satisfied the grown-ups were in charge. Next time he'd warn them about his precocious daughter.

"I'm sorry about that." Rafe smiled. "Where were we?"

Their food arrived, and he and Becca chatted. Pleasant enough conversation, even if he didn't particularly find the world of bridal wear fascinating.

"Would you like to go to my place after this?" Becca reached for his hand and stroked it. "I make a mean breakfast burrito."

Sex could be easy and available—at least that was what he'd heard from his buddies. Uncomplicated and temporary. That had only rarely been him, but casual might be all he could handle these days. Becca didn't set him on fire, but he wasn't exactly in the position to ask for the moon right now.

"Sure," he said, because damn it all, *two years*. It had been two *years*.

That was when his phone buzzed again, as if the universe had just informed Susan that her father was about to have a little adult fun.

"Sorry," Rafe said. "It might be my daughter."

"Again?" Becca said, voice dripping with annoyance.

"Yeah, she's…well, she's not taking the divorce well."

"Maybe you should put her in therapy."

Rafe bristled. He hadn't asked for Becca's advice. She wouldn't understand what it was like to raise a daughter while constantly afraid her mother was going to remember you weren't her biological father and pull the world out from under you.

"Hello," Rafe said briskly.

"Daddy?"

"Okay, honey, please give Cole his phone back and tell him to figure out a better password."

"I want a little sister."

Everything in Rafe stilled and he heard the sound of his own blood rushing through his veins. He made a motion to Becca that he'd be right back, stood and moved toward the back of the restaurant for a little privacy.

"What are you *talking* about, honey?"

"You and Mommy can have a baby just like Adam and Stacy did. I want a baby like Tennessee. She's so *cute*."

He dragged a hand through his hair. "Susan, a baby isn't like a dog. You can't just *get* one. And Mommy and I are *not* going to have a baby."

"But *why*?"

A thousand reasons were on the tip of his tongue, all inappropriate for a four-year-old.

Because she doesn't love me, and I don't love her.

Because we can't pretend to be a family anymore.

Because we both deserve better than a marriage in name only.

Because you're four and can't make these decisions. Because, because, because.

"Because. *That's* why."

"Sorry, Rafe," came Valerie's voice again, already sounding weary.

He was going to bring her a bag of salted caramel popcorn from the boardwalk and make chocolate pancakes every morning.

"That's okay. Just tell Cole he needs a better password."

Forcing himself to push thoughts of Susan's unacceptance of their reality, Rafe went back to Becca.

And she was gone.

"Yeah, I don't blame you," Rafe muttered.

It had been years since he'd been able to have a woman in his life, and even longer since a woman had been the center of his world. And Becca, like anyone, deserved better than what little Rafe had to offer.

He shook his head, settled the bill, then went to the bar to have a cold beer with Max.

Chapter Seven

Jordan changed again, pulled her hair into a pony-tail, removed her makeup, washed her face and prepared to retire for the evening. It was early, but she still had wedding favors to take apart and put back together. Many hundreds of times over. She swallowed hard and moved past the pebble of anxiety lodged in her throat. Rummaging through her suitcase, she searched for her chocolate stash. As if the wedding favor fiasco wasn't enough, she also had to talk sense into some genius Mensa doctor who loved jazz. And to top off the day, Rafe had waltzed in with a beautiful woman.

Hands down, today was made for chocolate. She broke off a square of delicious milk chocolate with toffee nuts and bit into it, closing her eyes to luxuri-ate in the rich sweet flavor.

Geoff hadn't checked in, texted or called other than when he'd phoned to say he wouldn't be com-ing to Texas at all. You know what? She didn't need him, either. She could, would and had been her own cheerleader for many years. Geoff helped mostly as a partner who assisted with her goal setting. He reminded her, frequently, not to lose focus, and *achieve, achieve, achieve.* They would someday be a power couple in California, and she had to keep her eyes on the prize.

But she never had any fun these days and won-dered if her sister Maribel could be right and Jordan had become a workaholic.

Thoughts of her sister sent her back to Susan, her sweet innocence and charm. Jordan wondered if she could move up her timeline for children. She made a mental note to ask Geoff his feelings on having children a bit earlier than their scheduled five years.

Somehow it didn't matter that Susan looked just like Liz. Something had split wide open in Jordan's heart the moment Susan had assured her not to be afraid. Jordan would love to bottle and sell the cour-age on that little girl. She'd started her life tragi-cally, but her luck had turned when Rafe stepped in to raise her.

The hour marched on and Jordan made good progress, ignoring how many hundreds more favors she had to do. In a pinch, she'd ask Maribel for help when she arrived in a few days with the rest of the family. They'd have an all-night girl talk session and get these done. Again, she was going above and beyond the call, but this was only one of the reasons her reputation had stretched far and wide. Attention to detail.

Finishing one more jewelry box ribbon and adding it to the growing pile, Jordan remembered to make a note about the flowers. She'd need to check on the vendor tomorrow, as they were again using someone local for obvious reasons. Jordan had a reliable list of vendors, but she'd had to make new relationships with a Texas wedding. It was all good. Just more networking for her, and in the future, she'd grow her business to involve destination weddings.

When her planner wasn't in her purse, Jordan didn't immediately panic. She had probably already pulled it out, so she searched the room. But the book wasn't on the dresser, in any of the dresser drawers or on the nightstand. It wasn't under the covers, or under the bed. She searched the room, panic swelling.

She must have forgotten it at the Bar and Grill, in her haste to leave before Rafe saw her.

She had everything that *mattered* written in her book. That book was her life!

Grabbing her purse, she rushed out the door.

"The date didn't go well?" Max set down another cold beer for Rafe.

"Susan called twice from Cole's phone. Going to have to talk to him about changing his password."

"Leave it to Kelly's daughter to figure it out. Next thing you know she'll be dismantling all her toys and putting them back together. They'll work better, too."

"Yeah, she might look like Liz, but she's Travis through and through. It's scary sometimes."

Max had met Special Ops Officer Lieutenant Travis Kelly before Susan had been born. Then, he'd been happily married to Lieutenant Liz Kelly, pilot. The two were an unstoppable team at one time. Max more than anyone else understood the sacrifice Rafe had made for Kelly. Rafe had been raised without a father. He couldn't just allow the daughter of the man who'd saved his life to grow up without one.

"You did good." Max met his gaze. "No one can fault you if it didn't work out between you."

"Yeah, well, I tried my best. I'm happy for Adam, though. Sometimes…it works."

"He's crazy about Stacy. It's true love."

And Rafe and Liz had never been in love.

But they'd certainly both been grieving at the same time. Liz, because she'd lost the love of her life. Rafe, who'd lost a good friend and thought he'd also lost Jordan for good. She'd been upset with the long deployments, and fed up, broken up with him. It hadn't been the first time she'd done something like that.

He'd thought it was one of their short fights, like the ones they'd had when he'd come back from a deployment and had a difficult time readjusting. She'd grow impatient with the short answers and he'd bite back with irritation.

But she hadn't returned any of his calls or texts for weeks, and he finally had to accept she was done with him. Shot down and finally giving up, he'd agreed to marry Liz. They'd both lost someone they loved, and they had Susan in common. The desire to give a little girl a whole family.

But he should have known better than to think it was over with Jordan. She'd been devastated when he'd told her his plans with Liz. Inadvertently, he'd fed Jordan's long held jealousies and insecurities about Liz.

To this day, Rafe viewed the way he'd handled it all with Jordan as his greatest personal failure.

Max got busy with some customers down on the other side of the bar, leaving Rafe to his thoughts. Jordan had moved on, and it was too late. She wouldn't care that she still made Rafe spark like the Fourth of July on steroids.

And speak of the devil, Jordan waltzed through the open doors of the Salty Dog. A man brushed by her, and as he not-so-discreetly lowered his gaze to check out her ass, Jordan moved to a bench where a couple was already seated. She began speaking to them in animated gestures. Were Rafe playing charades, he'd have to guess she was miming a book, as she held her palms out in the shape of an open one.

The couple stood, and together all three of them searched the seated area, and under the table. Rafe was going to step out on a limb and guess Jordan had lost a book of some kind. Maybe the one she'd clung to on the day of the dress fittings. Every time he'd caught her eye, she whipped out the book and scribbled something in it. He might not be Travis Kelly, but Rafe had also been at the top of his class. She'd used that book to avoid him.

While he didn't approve of Susan's description of Jordan, he had to acknowledge this new Jordan was a pent-up, tightly wound, type A, drill-sergeant type. This was the entire reason he'd dragged her along with him and Susan to the carousel. She needed to unwind. He could see she'd wanted an out from the invitation but was far too kind and well-mannered to be rude. Even to Liz's daughter, which said a lot about Jordan Del Toro. But nothing he didn't already know.

Jordan now took on a wild-eyed look and rushed to the back of the restaurant, passing right by him without even glancing his way. Tonight, she was dressed in tight stretchy black pants and a short T-shirt, her hair in a casual ponytail. This was the look he remembered, and it definitely still worked for him. Dressed this way, she would probably be unrecognizable to anyone in the wedding party. He understood she had an image to maintain. The look of a professional event planner. But while he wouldn't have put it in such crude terms, well, Susan had been right about the stick.

A few minutes later, she was back, still wild-eyed.

Rafe couldn't take it anymore. He was a single father in the business of finding lost wands, Barbies,
crayons and Lego. And he couldn't just stand by and
watch Jordan lose her collective shit.

"Hey," he said, putting himself in her way. She'd
have to notice him now.

"Rafe."

"I see you've lost something. Is it a book?"

"How did you know?"

"Charades. This is something special, I take it."

She met his eyes, hers shimmering with a suspicious wetness. "This book is my *life*. Everything is
in it. All my notes for the wedding, all the vendors.
All the dates."

"Okay, no problem. I'll help you look. Let's re-
trace your steps."

"I already did that."

"Humor me. Do it again."

She walked back to the booth where the couple
sat eating.

"I was sitting right here, talking to Ava for a while.
I had my book out, making some notes. Ava's father
loves jazz and wants a string quartet. Ava hates jazz.
Then she went back behind the bar to see Max." At
this point, she moved to the bar to demonstrate. "And
then, I…I…"

"What?" His gaze followed hers to the entrance
of the restaurant.

She shook her head. "Never mind. I saw something upsetting and got up to leave. I must have been distracted."

"And the book? Did you take it with you?"

"I thought I did! But I must not have, right? Who would take my planner? It doesn't make any sense. It's not expensive or has anything worthwhile in there to anyone else. Oh my God, I don't know what I'm going to do."

"Hey. Look at me." He tipped her chin and met her gaze. "Deep breaths. You're okay."

"No, I'm not. You don't understand. I *need* my book."

"Have you done a thorough check of your vehicle?"

"Of *course*."

"Do you mind if I double-check?" Rafe led the way outside and then followed Jordan to her rental. "I might as well be an expert in locating the unfindable. I've personally found pacifiers deep under seats when I was particularly desperate. They'd grown hair in the interim, but I just spit on it, and it works fine."

She made a disgusted face.

"I'm kidding," Rafe said after a beat.

But apparently, she'd forgotten he'd been a tactical explosives expert. In this case he wouldn't have to worry about blowing himself up, but he could slowly take apart entire systems and put them back together. He even removed the seats but didn't find anything the size of a book. He did, however, find a penny, a crayon, a dated gas receipt and an old and practically fossilized French fry.

"I'll go ask Max to check the lost and found. A waitress probably picked it up and put it in the back office."

"Oh, why didn't I think of that?"

"You're a little stressed out. Don't worry, I'm here to help. Didn't I ask you to use me in any way you want? Think of me as your assistant."

Suddenly, she reached up, a hand on each of his shoulders. The touch sent a jolt of awareness coursing through him. "Rafe. Please. Y-you can't tell Max."

"Can't tell him what?"

"Th-that I've lost my book. He has such faith in me. I don't want him to think he shouldn't have trusted me with his wedding day."

Something unnamed pinched Rafe's chest. He met her eyes and let his speak for him: *Don't be afraid. I'm here with you.*

"Don't worry. I won't say a word."

"Oh gosh, thank you, Rafe. *Thank* you." She went hand to chest.

"Why don't you go back to the hotel? This could take a while."

He didn't want to let her know he might have to resort to the dumpster. She'd be horrified at the thought.

"O-kay," she said slowly.

"Trust me, Zippy. I've got you."

Inside, Rafe asked Debbie, the head waitress, whether she'd seen his *watch*. She led Rafe to the back office, though she hadn't seen a watch. Fine, since he was searching for a book. No luck, anywhere, and Rafe didn't want to go look in the dumpster. Yet. At least when Susan was missing a Barbie doll, he'd never had to search the trash.

But after he'd made a sweep of the restaurant, including the men's bathroom, and discreetly asked a few of the staff if they'd noticed a stray book, Rafe saw no other way.

He reached for his cell and dialed Cole. "Hey, I'm going to be a little late. Is that all right?"

"Ah, it must be going well with Becca. Yeah, go ahead. Valerie got both Tennessee and Susan to sleep."

"Damn, she's a magician."

"Don't I know it. I was wicked smart to marry a teacher. Stay out as late as you want. You're owed a night of relaxation."

Yeah, not so much. He had a mission. It would be messy. Time-consuming. But should he succeed, he would get a genuine smile out of Jordan.

And how he'd missed that smile.

"Thanks, Cole." Rafe hung up.

He was going dumpster diving.

Chapter Eight

In her hotel room, Jordan continued the search for her planner. Under the bed. In the sheets, because she occasionally fell asleep while making notes.

Why did she still *cling* to the old ways? The only real answer was that she loved the feel of print, loved decorating her pages with bright, shiny stickers, making sketches. Each wedding had its own book, a little like its own fairy tale, and she had several of them at home on her bookshelf. With a wedding book, it felt like she was literally holding the future she wanted in her hands. It soothed her. Centered her. Tiny details were in the book. The details that made her weddings exceptional.

By the time she heard a knock on her door an hour later, she'd worked herself up into a frenzy. Max would lose faith in her. And Ava… Jordan wanted to disappoint her least of all. She was *the bride*. The Holy Grail in Jordan's metaphorical book. Print *or* digital.

Rafe stood on the other side of the door. "Sorry. No luck."

Earlier, he'd looked date-worthy. Swoony. Clean and presentable, wearing dark jeans and a blue button-up shirt rolled up to his elbows. Dressed to impress his lovely date. Now his hair was nearly as wild and unruly as her own.

"What *happened* to you?"

"I don't want to talk about it," he said, scowling.

"Come in." She waved him inside. "Where did you look? Did you tell anyone? Does Max know?"

"I told everyone I was looking for my watch. But I had zero luck. Not even in the dumpster."

"D-dumpster?"

Just the thought of her book among potato peels and God only knew what else… Yes, it was definitely hot in here. And there was no air. What kind of six-star hotel was this, anyway? Air was a necessity!

"I had to try." He shrugged. "I've literally looked everywhere. We have to face facts. Someone must have accidentally picked it up, thinking it was theirs, and taken it home with them."

Someone, out of the dozens of patrons there to-night. She couldn't even open her mouth to form words. Words became even scarcer when Rafe took her in his arms and pulled her close. Her face was nestled against his shoulder and for someone who'd been in a dumpster, he still smelled so good. A manly leather smell and divine cologne.

Which he'd worn for his date tonight.

As much as she was enjoying the embrace, Jordan pulled back. She was enjoying this a little too much. Rafe was no longer hers. Ancient history.

He squeezed her shoulders. "Eventually, it may take a couple of days, but they'll get the book back to you. Your name must be in it, right?"

"Y-yes."

"Until then, I've got a plan." He ran a hand through his hair and slid her an easy smile, which froze when he noticed the boxes cluttering her bed. "What's all this?"

"Wedding favors."

"*You're* making them?" He pointed to the ribbon and hot glue gun on the nightstand. "You really do it all, don't you?"

She shook her head. "They made a mistake and used a violet ribbon instead of a blue one."

He quirked a brow, then pulled one out of the box. "Is that important?"

"Yes, *Rafe*. It is. There's no time to send them back, so I'm taking care of it."

"By yourself?" He seemed to do a quick count of his own.

"I'll get it done. Don't worry. I feel like it's my mistake."

"*Your* mistake? How's that?"

"I should have ordered them much earlier, to account for an error like this." She covered her face. "I know better."

"Remember when I told you to think of me as your assistant?" He picked up a box. "I can help."

"You want to peel off violet ribbons and replace them with blue ones? It's detailed work."

He cocked his head. "Do you even *remember* what I did in the service?"

She rolled her eyes. "These aren't bombs."

"Makes it even easier. Listen. I can help."

"Fine!" She went palms up. "If you insist."

At this point, she was not stupid enough to turn down any help at all. Even from her ex-boyfriend, the man who smelled *too* good.

Rafe sat next to her, a box in his lap.

This made her move over, which meant nudging over another box. "What happened to your date tonight?"

He blinked. "How do you—"

Embarrassed, she tried to cover. "I made an assumption based on how nice you look."

And how good you smell.

"You think I look nice?" He sent her a slow smile.

"You *look* like you were on a date."

"I *was* on a date. She walked out on me."

"What? Why?"

"Happens all the time, though Becca moved fast. Most women don't appreciate that I'm a single father."

"That's crazy. Susan is adorable."

"Adorable and precocious. It's like she has a sixth sense of when I'm having any kind of fun without her. In fact, if she wasn't asleep, I'd be getting a phone call right now. So, I don't plan to introduce Susan to anyone until I'm serious with a woman. But the rules are different for me, anyway."

"What *rules*?"

"The dating rules. Remember, I'm not Susan's biological father. I have no rights now that we're divorced."

Jordan hadn't ever considered this. "But surely Liz wants Susan to have a relationship with the only father she's ever known."

"You would think so. Instead, she uses Susan as leverage to control me."

The thought made her wince. Liz, who'd always been smug and condescending toward Jordan the handful of times they'd met in the past.

"That's so wrong."

"She didn't want her to come with me on vacation and this is an in-state trip. I haven't been home to California with Susan since the divorce. Taking a trip with her out of state wouldn't happen without major negotiations."

"Your life is complicated." And would become even more so if and when Rafe ever fell in love with someone else. She almost felt sorry for the woman. "So, how *is* Liz?"

"She's dating someone. I think it's pretty serious."

"Well, then, I'm sorry. No hope of reconciliation?"

"Don't be sorry. I'm not. It's for the best."

"I'm sure Susan doesn't think so."

"Probably not, but she doesn't get to decide."

"It sounds like *Liz* got to decide." And the bitterness of that truth slid through her.

"No, it was mutual. Believe me. Let's go back to this other problem of yours. You can reconstruct everything you had in the book."

"Well, I wrote it down so I wouldn't *have to* rely on memory."

"But if you think about it, it's all still there, even further reinforced because you wrote it down." Rafe stood, walked over to the desk and reached for the hotel's pad and pen. "Let's go backward, step by step."

"Okay, look. I appreciate your mission-oriented personality but I'm not a *project*."

Ignoring her, he was already writing. "The last notes you took were about Ava's father and the jazz issue. So that's fresh on your mind. What kind of notes did you take?"

"Ava's father loves jazz. He wants to be involved, so I was going to find another way for him to contribute. And I have to make it seem as though it's *his* idea, not mine." She swiped her fingers in the air. "I drew a sketch of a musical treble for inspiration."

For the next few minutes, Rafe helped her reconstruct most of her recent pages in the book. And he was right. Most everything, all of the details, were still mostly in her head. She didn't have any of the fancy stickers she'd used on the pages, some of her sketches or cut-outs of bridal gowns. Maybe in some ways she'd come to rely on her planner like a crutch. But it comforted her, and there was nothing wrong with that.

Her assistant, Sherry, had backups of her backups. In the clouds. On external drives. Smart, and precisely what Jordan needed—someone more tech savvy than she'd ever been. But the notes she had in the book weren't on anyone's backup. They were those key touches that mattered to Jordan.

"Maybe you're right. I *can* reconstruct the book. And my assistant has all the phone numbers and contacts."

"You might want to put some of this on your phone."

"Yeah, yeah. Everyone lives by their phone."

"Not you?"

"I hate the way everyone is always staring at their phone. If you pay close attention, you'll notice couples, supposedly in love included, sitting at dinner reading their phones. Not talking to *each other*. This is one instance where my parents were right. Family time is key."

"It's one of the reasons I shut my phone off during dinner. I don't want Susan to grow up thinking that's normal." He cleared his throat. "Liz was always on her phone."

Jordan should have bristled at the mention of Liz's name, again, but instead she was focused on how often Geoff read his phone when they were having dinner. The news, text messages, work emails. She had considered instituting a similar rule but hadn't wanted to sound like a nag.

"I think it's disrespectful."

He nodded. "A time and a place."

They were both quiet for a moment, perhaps both remembering how much they'd once had in common. Rafe was raised by a single mother who worked long hours, and he'd often found his way to their home for family dinners. Her parents had practically thought of him as another son.

Then Rafe rubbed his hands together. "All right, let me at this gun."

How could anyone be this excited about helping her with wedding favors? Even Maribel would probably complain. "*I'll* work the glue gun. You can dismantle, since that's what you're good at, while I put them back together."

"You're the boss." He shrugged.

But despite her being the boss, it was Rafe who set up an assembly line. He removed ribbons like a surgeon and then passed the jewelry box to her. She carefully attached the blue ribbon to the box, using a dime-sized amount of glue. Occasionally, she used a little much, which was distressing.

"I want these to be perfect."

"Yeah, I got that." He smirked.

"Anything wrong with that? It's Max's wedding and I have a reputation to maintain. You should have heard Ava tonight. She said Max told her I'm the kind of person people come to with their problems."

"You almost sound surprised." He looked up from his work on another box. "I always thought so, too."

"You've *got* to be kidding me."

"I'm not."

"I did not have my act together a few years ago. I was restless, with zero direction. No solid plans."

He was kind enough not to mention her only direction had been him. She had used her born organizational skills to plan her life around Rafe's military service. When they spent time around other military couples, she learned how much the wives took on for their husbands. They were the backbone of the family and Jordan had planned to be that for Rafe. She'd planned her whole life around him, a dangerous thing.

"That's not how *I* remember you."

"Then I'm not sure who you're remembering." Satisfied with the new ribbon, she set it aside. "Someone else, I guess."

"Nope, I remember *you*. You always had a zest for life. You knew how to have a good time. Dancing. Cutting loose. Enjoying things I barely noticed."

"Maybe I wasted too much valuable time enjoying myself. I dropped out of phlebotomy school, then later nursing school. It wasn't until I finally found my skills with event planning that I found my purpose. I should have known. It goes back to my skills in having a good time and organizing. Remember, I planned all the parties. For my family. Our friends."

She remembered the "welcome home" party she'd organized for Rafe after a long deployment. Every time he'd come home felt like the first time. He'd hustle over to her, drop everything he was carrying and sweep her into his arms. His hugs were king-size and memorable. He'd made her feel loved, wanted and treasured, and he could do it with a single all-encompassing hug.

Her sister and all of her friends were jealous of what she had with Rafe.

"He *really* loves you. Everyone can tell."

Yeah, turned out, not so much. One horrible fight and a breakup she hadn't really wanted, and he found a future with someone else.

Jordan accidentally touched the hot glue and cursed. She brought her finger to her lips and flapped it in the air. "Damn it!"

"Let me see." Rafe took her hand, quickly inspected Jordan's finger, then gently led her to the bathroom basin, where he held her finger under ice-cold water.

"I'm okay. It's not bad at all," Jordan said, wanting to stop the gentle feeling brought about by Rafe taking care of her.

But he continued to carefully inspect her hand, and after a minute it felt like a caress. Unnerved by the pleasantness his touch brought about, she pulled her hand away. But the sudden jerky movement only made Rafe meet her eyes. They were close, far too close, and simply stared at each other for several interminable seconds. For Jordan, the air was thick and charged between them. It felt like before, all those times when they'd hardly been able to keep their hands off each other.

But she wasn't going to fall for Rafe. Not again. She was way too smart for that.

Finally, he broke the silence. "I… I should go."

"Yes." She took a deep breath and walked with him to the door. "But thank you for your help tonight. I must have seemed like an out-of-control junkie earlier. That's not the real me."

He canted his head. "You were fine. It's completely understandable."

"I'm sure you've never lost your cool like that over something so…*replaceable*."

"A few times, actually." He met her gaze, or tried to, but she glanced away quickly.

"I have a difficult time believing it."

"All *things* are replaceable. But not people."

She wanted to believe that, but he'd replaced *her*, with Liz. It had only taken him a few weeks, too. And it hurt to this day to realize how expendable she'd been. How quickly he'd moved on.

He stopped in the doorframe, just inches from her. "Jordan, *look at me*."

Reluctantly, she raised her eyes to meet his gaze. "Yes?"

"You're not replaceable. And I missed the hell

out of you." With that, he turned and walked out the door without a backward glance.

The simple words, the ease with which he'd uttered them, stunned her to the core. She stood immobile for several seconds, then shut the door slowly, wondering if she could have *heard* right.

Suddenly, the lost planner was the least of Jordan's problems.

Chapter Nine

"Daddy, look! Look! It's a mermaid," Susan cried, pointing to the crashing waves.

He made a mock attempt to see said mermaid and shielded his eyes from the bright sun. "Where?"

"Right there! *I* think it's Ariel." She went skipping along ahead of him, Sub following loyally behind.

Even a walk along the private beach adjacent to the lighthouse couldn't clear Rafe's head. A few days later, he couldn't get his mind off the words he'd said to Jordan.

You idiot.

Jordan had moved on and done well for herself. The damage was done, irreparable, and he shouldn't complicate her life or his own. The custody arrangement and the peace he'd brokered with Liz was tenuous at best. Jordan remained a sore point to Liz and only one of the many reasons she'd resisted this vacation. She liked to throw her weight around and remind him Susan was not *his*. Remind him that on some level she would always control him.

But he couldn't simply stand and discuss the replaceable and the *irreplaceable* without remembering that on some level, Jordan believed he'd replaced *her*.

It wasn't true, of course. The only thing that had him going through with the wedding to Liz was a willing sacrifice for his fallen brother. Protecting Kelly's widow and baby was the very least Rafe owed the man who'd saved his life. He'd listened to Liz when she told him that Kelly would have wanted it this way, all three of them together. Married. A little family. He regretted the hubris that had allowed him to believe he could somehow make it work.

But he was no longer filled with endless confidence and a rigid mentality. He was a parent. He now operated under the assumption that whatever could go wrong often did. Plans were simply a guideline. A budget was a mere suggestion. A job was a way to make enough money to survive and not a way to confirm his self-worth. The list went on.

He'd once had high achiever goals and slayed one right after the other. With a plan in place, he and Jordan were working toward their future. He'd rise through the ranks, and once he'd reached lieutenant and the pay increase it came with, he and Jordan would marry and have the children they'd both wanted. She'd agreed to follow him all over the country and the world, packing up the household as often as needed.

Then a bomb had *literally* blown up, taking a good man out of the world. Years later, Rafe still felt the damage it had inflicted reverberating through his life. The explosion that took Kelly's life had taken Rafe's as well. The electric waves had left him the only father to a little girl who loved him unconditionally.

Thankfully, Susan had forgotten all about her urgent need for a baby sister when she'd woken this morning. Apparently, out of sight, out of mind when it came to Tennessee, who'd gone home with her parents. He'd have a talk with Susan later about him and Liz reconciling. And though she'd been rude, Rafe considered whether Becca had been right, and his little girl might need counseling to move past the divorce.

The thought stung but he'd do anything for Susan. Because a reunion with Liz was never going to happen, especially after once again being front and center with real love. With the way it gripped him and wouldn't let go. He couldn't resist touching Jordan when he was near her, had barely resisted kissing her last night. But she was with someone and he could not intervene with that.

Tonight, he'd have another chance to make a fool out of himself at the wedding rehearsal dinner, held at the Salty Dog. The entire establishment would shut down for the evening as Max hosted. Rafe had assumed he'd have to take Susan along but a group of senior citizens calling themselves the Almost Dead Poet Society had stepped up and volunteered to watch both Susan and Tennessee.

A few hours later, he'd enjoyed hours of sandcastle building, mermaid sightings through the lighthouse's telescope and playing fetch with Sub. Rafe felt a pinch of guilt at how much he was looking forward to being away from Susan for the evening. He loved his little girl, but sometimes, damn, she was…a lot. For her entire life, he'd deprived himself of those small things he enjoyed, like getting out occasionally. Meeting the guys for a cold beer, dancing, going to the movies to make out with a beautiful woman. And yeah, all the stuff which came *after* a great make-out session.

"When will you be back?" Susan bounced on his bed as he adjusted his tie.

"You'll be asleep when I get back."

"*That* long?" She cocked her head as if he'd explained he'd be gone for a hundred years.

"It's going to be late, and past your bedtime."

"Who's going to read me my stories?"

"Valerie's grandmother and all her friends will be here. I heard they love reading. They even have story time at the bookstore. I'll have to take you sometime."

"Well," she said, adopting a tone of voice that always made her sound so much wiser than her four years. "If we have time. We have to get back home soon."

"I thought you were having a good time here."

Too late, Rafe realized Susan had simply parroted Liz's words. They'd talked on the phone yesterday and those words sounded like Liz's words. Susan was her mini-me most days.

"Mommy says we have to come back home. You *have* to bring me home."

Rafe's head jerked back in surprise. "Of course, I'm taking you home."

"We can't stay here forever. That's what Mommy says."

He bristled with irritation. Liz once again reminding him who was in control. This time through their daughter.

"Mommy is right. We don't live here. That's why it's called a *vacation*."

"But I really like it here. I told Mommy you, me and her should live in a lighthouse by the beach. And I can have a dog."

At least she'd forgotten about the baby.

"Dallas is pretty far from the beach."

Susan sighed, sounding so much like Liz that for a moment he winced. "That's what Mommy says."

"Tell you what. We'll come back here another time, too. Maybe before you start kindergarten."

Susan's eyes widened in happy surprise. Charming was a difficult place not to fall in love with.

* * *

When Valerie's grandmother arrived, she had cookies with her. "I heard there's a little girl here who loves cookies."

"Me, me, me!" Susan came careening down the staircase.

Valerie took the tray of cookies from her grandmother and carried them into the kitchen. "After dinner, right?"

"I made mac and cheese." Rafe pointed to the covered pan of Susan's favorite meal.

"Are you going to tell me a story?" Susan pointedly asked Mrs. Villanueva. "Daddy said you were going to tell me stories."

"Yes, *mijita*. I will tell you many stories." Mrs. Villanueva tousled Susan's hair. "Just like the ones I told Valerie when she was little."

"Okay, because I like *a lot* of stories."

When Adam and Stacy arrived with Tennessee, Susan ran upstairs and came back with her wand. "Now I can turn her into a princess!"

"She's going to love that," Stacy said as she settled her daughter down in the portable crib Adam had set up.

Adam had also brought with them another member of the poetry group, their neighbor Susannah Ferguson, who introduced herself to Rafe.

"How nice to meet one of Adam's little friends," she said.

"Say hello, my little friend." Rafe chuckled and he and Adam fist-bumped.

Shortly thereafter, the room filled with more senior citizens. Eventually, Rafe lost track of the names as he was introduced.

"Don't worry," Roy Fink, the only man among them, explained. "Between all of us we've raised twenty children and have a collective thirty-five grandchildren."

"That's…a lot," Rafe said.

"I know what kids today are doing," Roy said, holding up his phone. "And I have an app for that."

"Do me a favor? Keep your phone close."

After a few minutes of saying their goodbyes, all five were out the door, Rafe being the proverbial fifth wheel. He'd been the one forced to rent a van at the car rental agency, so he was automatically the designated driver. Cole sat in the front passenger seat, Valerie behind him for the extra room she needed for her expanding belly. In the back passenger seat of his rental, Stacy and Adam were joking about their "shotgun" wedding.

At the rehearsal, Jordan went through the routine once, explaining how this would all go, and the second time she added herself into the mix.

At the back of the church, about to go through the run-through one last time, Jordan's sister took Rafe aside.

"How's married life, *guapo*?"

It had been Maribel's childhood nickname for him and meant "handsome" in Spanish.

"Divorced," he said without missing a beat.

"That was quick."

"Funny, it didn't feel quick."

"Ah, one of those. Well, sorry. Especially since Jordan moved on. You're like a dot in the distance now."

"I didn't *cheat* on her, Maribel," he said through a clenched jaw.

"Yes, that's what you said."

He would expect that kind of allegiance to Jordan and it didn't bother him. Everyone, Jordan included, incorrectly assumed he'd cheated with Liz. He never had and when he saw Jordan one last time before he married Liz, he'd told her that. She'd never believed him. And marrying Liz was not the best way to prove he'd never been unfaithful to Jordan.

If he expected Jordan to treat him any differently after his confession, he was wrong. Mostly, she was acting as if none of it had happened. She treated him like any other groomsman, ordering him around like a little dictator. They were all to move precisely to the beat of the music, a very slow march down the aisle.

Someone kill him, please.

"Rafe, please remember that Valerie's legs aren't as long as yours. Slow your roll. It's not a race to the finish line."

"I went to war against people like you," Rafe muttered before he went down the aisle for the third time.

"Huh?" She gave him a puzzled look.

He shook his head. "Never mind."

Finally, after Jordan had adequately put everyone through their paces, even ordering Ava's father around, telling him to "loosen up," and "unkink those shoulders," they all headed to the restaurant for dinner.

Chapter Ten

"Damn, this looks like a regular Friday night when we're slammed," Cole joked as Rafe pulled into the parking lot.

Inside, the place was transformed with four long, cloth-covered tables decorated with rosebud vases and a tapered candle. The DJ Rafe had ordered was setting up in a corner.

"Who ordered the DJ?" Stacy asked.

"That was me." Rafe held up his finger. "You can't have a real party without a DJ."

"You're dancing with me tonight." Stacy threw her arms around Adam's neck.

"Of course, I am." Adam kissed his wife, then led her to a table.

"Let's you and I sit together," Maribel said to Rafe.

"The DJ was a nice touch and totally not necessary. I forgive you for being an idiot."

"Thanks."

He had a way to go with the rest of the family, especially given the scowls on Mr. and Mrs. Del Toro's faces. If looks could kill, he'd be maimed. Still, he'd been through far worse, and nodded politely in their direction with a tight smile.

Rafe held the chair out for Maribel, seating them at a Del Toro table with Max's parents and other siblings.

"This night is going to be such fun for you." Maribel smirked.

"Yeah. I'm having a blast."

"If Jordan forgave you, I can. It happened. She broke up with you, you married Liz in four short weeks. But that's okay now. She found Geoff and they're happy. My parents are going to be a little harder to win over, of course. You know how invested they were in the two of you."

Now that he had a daughter, he understood far more than *anyone* realized. If a man ever hurt Susan the way he had Jordan, they'd wind up missing vital organs. He considered himself grateful to be among the living with any Del Toro in the crowd. Many of them didn't know he was divorced, or they'd probably be dancing in the streets that his marriage had failed.

Out of the corner of his eye, Rafe observed Jordan flitting about. He wondered if she'd even sit down to have the meal. Then again, Max, Cole and Adam were also not seated, probably first checking that everything in the kitchen was running smoothly. They had their full staff working tonight, and for the evening, their relief bartender behind the bar. Mr. Del Toro was already over there, presumably medicating himself.

Rafe wished he could join him, but he was the designated driver, a good role for a single dad that didn't get out much.

The food was delicious, a mixture of Tex-Mex and Latin-inspired dishes that reminded Rafe of home. And a good reason not to engage in pointless conversations. Rafe went with it. He fervently wished to be seated at the Long table, where friendly and outgoing Lucia held court. Rafe checked his cell to confirm there were no messages. So, either there were no phones in sight to hijack, or maybe Susan was thoroughly entertained.

"I'm going to go check in with the DJ." Rafe stood and excused himself.

This had nothing to do with the fact that Jordan seemed engaged in a spirited conversation with him. The DJ handed her a card.

"Hey," Rafe said to the DJ. "Are you all set?"

Jordan turned to Rafe. "Did you know we need a DJ for the reception?"

"I didn't."

"Apparently Dr. Long canceled the one I'd booked when he hired the string quartet." Jordan frowned.

"I tried to get them back, but they'd already booked another date."

"Fortunately, I'm available," the DJ said.

"I can't tell you how much I appreciate this." Jordan gave the man a wide smile. "One less thing on my list."

"Anything for you, sweetheart." The man winked.

A jealousy Rafe had no right to feel flared and burned in his gut. "What about the favors?" Rafe took Jordan aside. "I'll help."

"You don't have to. Maribel is here now. I know you're busy with your daughter. You should enjoy your vacation."

"I am. Mostly."

He threw a look at the table where Mr. and Mrs. Del Toro were seated, currently shooting daggers in his direction. He was probably never supposed to talk to Jordan again and certainly not stand this close to her.

Jordan followed his gaze. "I'll talk to them. Don't let any of that worry you. You're welcome here. Max wanted you as his best man, which has nothing to do with my parents."

"So…tough luck for them?"

"Just give them a little time. They're reasonable people."

"That's what I'm afraid of. I think your father has already picked out my casket."

She blinked. Jordan was never fond of gallows

humor. "Look. I don't want you to worry or think about what you said to me the other night."

"When I said I missed you?"

She cleared her throat and looked around to make sure no one had heard. "Yes, *that*. I realize you might have spoken in a moment of weakness. A divorce is tough and it's only natural to have regrets."

And…there it was. Leave it to Jordan to give him a graceful way out. To let him know he had a chance to take his words back without repercussions.

He couldn't do it. "No. I meant every word. I'd like to add, too, that I've missed you for four years. And I still miss you."

"Rafe," she said between gritted teeth. *"Don't."*

"Just being honest." He held up both palms.

"I don't have time for this. I have to… I have to…" Before he could say another word, she went off to check in with Max.

"Yeah, you go ahead and do that," Rafe muttered to himself.

"Ahem," a decidedly feminine voice said from behind him.

He turned to see Maribel carrying two drinks. She held one out for him.

"Thanks, but I can't. Designated driver. And father of one. Best man and bridesmaid's ex. Plus, to some people, such as myself, a tool."

"Oh, well. More for me." She took a sip from one of the drinks with a parasol in it. "I overheard what you were saying just now."

"Eavesdropping? I thought you got over that in seventh grade."

"Don't be an idiot. I'm here to help."

"Sounds too good to be true so I'm going to say no. But thanks."

"Aw, Rafe. I knew this would happen someday. You'd feel sorry for leaving Jordan and come crawling back."

"Don't forget she left *me*." He cleared his throat. "And I'm not crawling."

"Well, you will be." She slid him an evil smile from behind the parasol. "If you ever want to make any progress."

"Great." His eyes followed Jordan, now consulting with Cole, and pointing toward the bar. "And why do you want to help me, exactly?"

"Long story short, I don't like Geoff."

"Yeah?"

A hopeful development. In the back of his mind, he'd considered whether perhaps this "almost" engagement of Jordan's wasn't even a real thing. The calculating part of his officer training had a different take. He respected commitments and loyalties more than most, but until she had a ring on her finger, all options were open.

"Geoff is too invested in his career, like someone else I remember. And I've always thought she could do better than him."

"I'm probably not better."

"You've changed." She bumped his shoulder. "If you want, I'll help you."

"Thanks, but I'm a big boy."

The last thing he needed was Maribel putting in a good word for him. Jordan would assume it had all been his idea. Despite what Maribel said, Rafe would not *crawl*. He'd lost a lot of pride through sleepless nights, an unhappy marriage and Susan's colic and teething. Best hang on to whatever he had left for a rainy day.

They breezed through dinner, the two dining tables separated and distinct but somehow still a part of each other. On one side, a family of physicians. On the other, working-class folks like Rafe. Lucia served as an almost literal bridge between their two worlds.

What Rafe wouldn't give for a bridge back to the past. When he hadn't made the worst decision of his life. He'd learned the hard way some sacrifices were too big. Funny, because his own life he would have given up for Travis Kelly in a heartbeat, but living a lie had been too much to ask.

"All right, everybody. The best man hired me to liven up this party," the DJ announced. "Let's get some bodies moving tonight. This is a celebration."

"Celebration," the song, blared out from the speakers. Rafe threw a brief glance in the direction of the Long family table and found that Ava's brothers, the other Dr. Longs in the family, were already making their way to the area designated for dancing, their wives in tow. Lucia tugged on Ava's father, while Ava's mother laughed and waved them both away.

This gave Rafe the perfect opportunity to ask Ava's mother to dance.

"I'm Rafe, the best man." He held out his hand. "May I have the honor?"

"Of course." She stood and accepted his hand on to the small square of space cleared for a dance floor. "You're Max's childhood friend, is that right?"

"Yep, we grew up together. I've never seen Max happier in his life. If you want to know the truth, he's always been a bit of a grump. Looks like Ava fixed him."

"We're thrilled. Our Ava hasn't always made the best choices, but this is a good one."

Before the song ended, Ava's father, with his perfectly trimmed goatee and silver hair, cut in to dance with his wife. This left Rafe to dance with Lucia.

Though she was probably around the same age as Ava's parents, her latte skin was mostly smooth of wrinkles. She also wore bright colors he most often saw on younger women, and several shiny bracelets on each wrist. Her only concession to aging seemed to be her salt-and-pepper hair. She could be either forty or sixty. He had no idea.

"Are you having a better time now?" Lucia asked as he led her around the dance floor.

"Not much, thanks. It's tough to have a good time

while someone plans your early demise." He threw a significant glance in the direction of Jordan's father, dancing a few feet away from him with his wife, glaring at Rafe.

Lucia's gaze followed. "I see. *Madre de Dios*, what on earth did you ever do to the man?"

"I didn't marry his daughter."

Lucia blinked. "Did you leave her at the altar?"

Rafe chuckled. "Oh, no. No, I don't think I'd be standing here having this conversation with you if I had. At least not with all four limbs intact."

More gallows humor but Lucia seemed to take it in stride. "This sounds like an intriguing story."

"Not really. Let me ask you this. Have you ever done a good deed that wound up costing you far more than you ever expected to give?"

Lucia nodded, her dark eyes sage and knowing. "*Mijo*, that's the best kind."

Rafe let that opinion settle over him. Obviously, he didn't agree.

The song over, they traded partners with Ava and Max.

A few more twirls around the dance floor with several partners and Rafe wound up face-to-face with Stacy.

Adam wanted to dance with his wife again and switched with Rafe.

This left Jordan front and center.

"Should we?" He held out his hand.

"It would be weird if we didn't."

The DJ switched to a slower tune. Score! Rafe pulled Jordan close, hip to hip, assuaging any lingering guilt by reminding himself of Maribel's words.

Chapter Eleven

Jordan took both of Rafe's hands and pulled them up to her waist since they lingered a little too low on her hips. Dangerously close to her behind, actually, and she wasn't going to allow that kind of casual familiarity. Frankly, she *was* enjoying watching Rafe squirm under her parents' frosty glares. It helped that, as usual, he was a feast for the eyes tonight, and she didn't mind feasting. Her eyes weren't in a committed relationship.

Whether dressed in fatigues, board shorts or a suit, Rafe had a way of walking into a room and commanding everyone's attention with his presence. Tonight, he'd cleaned up well. Freshly shaved, with only the slightest hint of beard stubble. But his chocolate brown hair curled at his neck, giving him a boyish look. There were tiny crinkles on the sides of his eyes when he smiled, and a furrow between his brows she'd never noticed before, reminding her he was no longer a boy.

By all outward appearances, Rafe had it all. Personality, intelligence, success and don't forget those smoldering Latin good looks. Now, for the topper, he was a father devoted to his daughter. He probably had to beat the women off with a stick.

"Your father has his laser eyes focused. I'm in his scope. You're loving this, aren't you?" Rafe lowered his gaze to meet hers.

"Love might be too strong a word." She quirked a brow for the double entendre she'd lobbed at him. "I would say I'm *enjoying this*. And I'd forgotten what a great dancer you are."

"How could you forget? We took lessons together."

Right. Lessons for the wedding she'd dreamed of one day. The one that never was.

He dipped her and kept her there a second too long, pulling a laugh out of her.

"Show-off."

She'd *laughed*. Another one of her walls came tumbling down, because hey, when he was big enough to own up to missing her… He might just have some regrets, and she should accept it. Maybe. What else did she want from the man? She was past the point of wanting him to bleed and cry. And they couldn't both hop in a time machine. It had all happened, and she hoped, for a reason. In her case, at least, she'd grown up.

"Tell me you don't miss us," Rafe said. "The way we were together."

"Of course I miss us. I'm not going to lie."

"We were good together."

"*Before.* Maybe because… I don't know, sometimes I think a part of me liked being in your shadow. You were like the sun for me. I felt safe there. Protected. But I never found my own way until you were out of my life."

He blinked, and the emotion crossing his features could be called nothing but pain. "You think I held you back?"

"No, I'm not saying that. Maybe I held *myself* back."

She had planned to be a military wife, following the sun wherever he went.

"You would have found your way, whether we stayed together or not."

"But we didn't. Anyway, I forgave you a long time ago."

"Liar."

"We were both to blame. Look, I'm sorry it took a divorce to make you realize you made a mistake. I wish you would have figured that out years ago."

"That's the thing about a mistake. You don't always know when you're about to make one. Remember, you gave up on us."

She considered her own emotional feelings regarding Travis, Liz and Rafe. She'd felt excluded by their powerful connections. And then she'd lashed out in anger and fear. Had she known she'd lose Rafe permanently, maybe she wouldn't have ignored him when he'd obviously tried to reconcile. That would remain her mistake, and no, she didn't know she'd made it until after the fact. Call it one of the mistakes of youth.

The music sped up and Rafe spun her and dipped her once again. Jordan came up laughing. Then she turned in Rafe's arms, and there at the entrance of the Salty Dog was none other than Geoff.

"Oh my gosh."

"What is it?" Rafe followed her gaze.

"That's…that's Geoff. He's actually here." She lowered her hands from Rafe's neck to his shoulders and stopped moving.

Rafe followed her lead, releasing her. "You should probably go say hello, then."

"Yes, I should." Leaving Rafe on the dance floor, Jordan rushed to meet Geoff. "You made it."

He bussed a chaste kiss on her lips. "It wasn't easy, but I know how important this whole thing is to you."

This whole thing? This was her brother's *wedding*.

"Thank you for making the time." Gosh, she sounded so disgustingly grateful to him for sparing her a moment.

"Of course." Geoff's eyes followed Rafe, now talking to Lucia. "Who's that you were dancing with?"

"That's Rafe."

"*Rafe?* Hopefully his wife is not the jealous type. Luckily, I'm not, because you two looked quite cozy there."

"We weren't *cozy*. Just dancing. And he's…divorced."

Geoff's eyebrows furrowed. "And are you happy about that?"

"Of course not. Why would I be? Here, come with me. Let me introduce you to Ava's family." She took his hand and led him around for introductions to the people he hadn't already met.

Ava's entire family. Then Cole, Valerie. Adam and Stacy.

The introduction to Rafe was by far the toughest. "Rafe, this is Geoff, my…my…"

"Fiancé." Geoff shook Rafe's hand.

"Congratulations." Rafe met Geoff's eyes, giving only a quick sideways glance to Jordan.

So Geoff was claiming her. Right here, right now, in front of the one man she'd wanted to eat crow for years. She'd wanted Rafe to have regrets. Wanted him to suffer the way she'd suffered when he chose Liz. But funny, it didn't feel the way she'd always hoped.

A completely unexpected ache wound its way around her heart as if *she* were the one being punished.

"Nice to meet you. If you'll excuse me." Rafe then made his way to the bar to join Cole.

Geoff snorted. "He seems nice. Glad I showed up before he got any ideas."

"Rafe wouldn't do that. He respects commitments."

Which meant he'd likely *never* cheated on her as she'd once believed. On some basic level, she'd known all along. He'd tried to tell her, but her jealous and obstinate mind wouldn't listen. Liz, Travis and Rafe were a cozy trio. And then Travis was gone. Rafe was suddenly spending a lot of time with Liz, planning a memorial, dealing with the US military and Travis's Medal of Honor.

It had been such a difficult time that even now, Jordan felt the profound sense of loss as if it had happened yesterday.

"Oh, hey there," Maribel said, coming up to them. "You actually *made* it."

"I wouldn't miss this," Geoff said, bringing Jordan's hand to his lips and kissing it. With the other, he scrolled through his cell. "Any food left for me?"

"The food is for the wedding party and immediate family," Maribel said. "You actually weren't invited to this. You're supposed to come to the *wedding.* Along with everyone else."

Frankly, it *was* rather rude of Geoff to drop in unannounced. Jordan should be happier to see him because at least he'd made the time to come for part of the festivities.

"I can't be at the wedding itself as I explained to Jordan. But I'm here now."

"Oh, well. Great!" Maribel slowly clapped her hands. "Fan-tas-tic."

It was no great secret that Maribel was not Geoff's

greatest fan. She considered him arrogant, aloof and entitled. And, well, maybe he was. A little. But he'd pulled Jordan out of a dark place and she was forever grateful.

"Cut it out, Maribel," Geoff said, voice dripping with irritation. "I have a lot of responsibilities as a trial lawyer. You have *no* idea."

"Right." She pointed to her temple. "This little head can't hold much information inside. Just my PhD dissertation and that's about it. I'm full now."

"Why don't we just leave and get something to eat somewhere in town?" Jordan interrupted before this escalated.

Besides, if she spent a little time with Geoff tonight, she'd remember why she loved him and what she liked about him. She'd be happier to see him instead of feeling like he'd interrupted a moment with Rafe.

Because...*that* was crazy.

Jordan checked in with Max and Ava, then said her goodbyes to the family.

"Thank goodness Geoff showed up," her mother said. "We were beginning to worry. You and Rafe, dancing. Bad idea, *mi amor.*"

"Si," her father grunted.

"I can't dance with the man you once thought of as a son?"

"You weren't dancing with him the way you dance with your brothers." Mami's lips went tight with disapproval.

Hard to argue with that one. She lowered her head and kissed her mother's cheek. "Don't worry, okay?"

As usual, Maribel had her two cents and pulled Jordan aside before she left. "Are you okay?"

"Of course. Why?"

"Because…I saw you with Rafe."

"Oh my gosh, not you, too. We were dancing right along with everyone else. You danced with him, too. No big deal."

Maribel rolled her eyes. "He doesn't look at anyone else the way he does you. And now, he's divorced."

"I'm not going to fall right back into his arms because he's suddenly free. Besides, his life is complicated. Liz still tries to control him with her daughter. I'm especially sensitive to that as you can imagine."

"All I'm saying is, be sure you're really done with Rafe before you marry Geoff."

Jordan usually respected her sister's advice, a good thing since Maribel had majored in psychology and was now a social worker. *And* an amateur psychiatrist. She'd psychoanalyzed Geoff to be a narcissist.

Instead of telling Maribel that she already realized she was done with Rafe, she said something else entirely. "Rafe said he missed me every day for four years."

Maribel quirked a brow. "That marriage was doomed from the beginning. It was entirely one-sided."

Maybe. But yes, Jordan would be sure not to have any feelings left for Rafe before she married Geoff.

Because she couldn't imagine being in a marriage when she longed for someone else.

Jordan drove to a restaurant on the other side of town. All the while, Geoff scrolled through his phone, thumbs flying from time to time as he texted someone. Or replied to an email.

"Idiot," Geoff muttered. "He thinks we're going to let our client accept his lowball offer."

Inside the Crescent Moon Restaurant, Geoff ordered dinner, making the waitress come back twice when the steak wasn't cooked to his satisfaction.

"You'd think here in Texas, they'd know how to cook a steak."

Jordan cringed. She always smoothed things over with the waitstaff, and she did so again now, apologizing profusely.

And Geoff was still scrolling through his cell.

"Um, Geoff? What's so important it can't wait a minute while we eat?"

He scowled, then finally put the phone down. "The game scores. And my colleague is texting me because he's a sore winner."

"Well. I wanted to talk to you about something." She swallowed thickly. "Why do you think I...we... haven't set a date for our wedding?"

"We've both been busy. But we should really do that, babe." He patted her hand. "Soon."

"Because I was thinking you never actually *asked* me. Not officially."

"Yes, I did."

"No, you didn't." She held up her ring finger to demonstrate.

This went right over Geoff's head.

"Jordan," he said, looking up at the ceiling as if trying to locate his misplaced patience. "Remember, we were sitting at breakfast one morning and I said, 'Do you think we should get married?' And you said yes, we should."

She briefly recalled the moment, two years ago, when she thought she had everything she'd ever wanted in her life.

A blossoming career, a solid relationship and a serious commitment to a great guy.

To a pretty good guy.

To a *guy*.

"But we kind of left it there. Didn't we?"

"Like I said, we've both been busy with our careers. And that's important."

"Yes, but I plan weddings for a *living*."

"Exactly, it's like a chef who doesn't like coming home to cook for their family." He chuckled at his lame joke. "Understandable."

"It's not like that. I love weddings. I've dreamed of planning my own nearly half of my life."

And why haven't I? What am I waiting for? Why don't I set a date? He'd probably go along with it. What's stopping me?

"Then why don't you get on with it? Oh, wait, I get it." He picked up his cell and began to scroll. "And you're right. I'll need to clear the decks. So do you, but your schedule is more flexible obviously.

Your clients can get married any time of the year. Let me see here. No, that won't work. Okay, there's June… Nope, there's not. Let's see here. Well, that's pretty amazing. It looks like June fifth, two years from now, is completely *open*. Let's do it, babe! Let's get married!"

Jordan gaped. "You want to marry me two *years* from now?"

"Why? Does that date not work for you?"

Jordan struggled to put her thoughts into words. This wasn't *about* setting a wedding date. It wasn't about Geoff, and it *wasn't* about Rafe. This was about her, damn it, and she deserved *better* than a man who had to fit her into his schedule. She deserved someone who loved her enough to be passionate now and again. Who couldn't wait to be with her and start their life together.

Oh, Jesus. She couldn't believe this. But instead of pain or fear, a slam of excitement went through her. She was about to claim her life back.

"I'm afraid there's another reason I haven't set a date. A more important one." She reached for his hand. "This isn't going to work for me. I clearly *don't* want to marry you."

Chapter Twelve

"I thought I would be sadder than this," Jordan said.

"And I thought I would be happier." Maribel shrugged. "Go figure."

Jordan had expected to feel *something*, at least, and imagined it all might hit later. When she wasn't this busy. Maybe when she went home, the loneliness would strike and she'd miss Geoff. Then she'd cry and wonder if she'd done the right thing breaking up with him.

She regretted the last time she made a snap decision about a man, but somehow this one felt…right.

For now, her thoughts were a jumble with memories of how many times he'd let her down. How many excuses she'd made for him over the years because she'd been afraid to be alone. And in every sense of the world's definition, Geoff was a great catch. Handsome, financially established, single and by his account, ready for marriage. Too bad he couldn't fit a wedding into his *schedule*.

She and Maribel were sitting in Jordan's hotel room, having once again set up the same assembly line Rafe had with ribbons, jewelry box and glue gun. This time Jordan was removing the ribbons while Maribel used the glue gun.

"I didn't end things because of Rafe. And it wasn't because I was worried I'd be thinking about Rafe after I married Geoff. I'm *already* thinking about Rafe."

"Totally understand."

"This doesn't mean I'm going to *take up* with Rafe again."

Maribel snorted. "Hardly."

"He doesn't deserve me, *either*."

"Does any man? Papi would say no."

"You forget he used to adore Rafe."

"Which is probably equal in strength to his hatred for him now." Maribel set the glue gun down and rubbed her neck. "I wish you weren't so attentive to detail. This isn't how I pictured spending wedding week. I'm single and I'd like to have a little beach fun while I'm here."

"I appreciate your help. This is a disaster."

"Your idea of a disaster and mine are *so* different. You really need to learn to ask for help from other people. *Besides* me."

"You're my only sister. It's your cross to bear."

"Did you ever consider this could also be *your* time to unwind? I mean, you just cut Geoff loose. Time to find out who else is out there."

"So soon? When I have our brother's wedding coming up? Are you insane?"

"What I am is young and free. And even I can see that Rafe is still a catch."

"He's ancient history. With all that happened between us, it would never work a second time."

"It doesn't have to work. How about a fling?"

"With *Rafe*?"

"Unless there's someone else that you find attractive and available. Facts are, no matter what Rafe did or didn't do, he's someone you can trust with your body. In other words, we all know him. He's not a serial killer."

"Wow. Such high standards. As long as he's not a *serial killer* he's a good choice for a fling?"

Jordan might be able to trust Rafe with her body but *not* her heart. And those two were forever entwined. It was fine for other people to have flings, and she didn't spend her time judging and moralizing. But not her. She wasn't built that way.

"I don't *do* flings."

"You're just saying that because you never had one."

"And I'm sure not going to start now, right before Max's epic wedding day."

Maribel sighed and set aside another box. "I think

we should call in some extra help. All we need is a few more hands and we'll crank these out in a few hours."

"Fine, but I'm not asking Rafe again. It's hard enough to be around him and I don't want him in my hotel room again."

"Let's go to the lighthouse and get Valerie's help. She's a teacher. What are the odds she's worked on craft projects before?"

Jordan was a bit embarrassed she hadn't thought of it herself. And surely Valerie wouldn't judge.

"I didn't want to bother anyone else in the wedding party."

"Just me?" Maribel squeaked. "Ask yourself if that's fair only because we're related. I bet Valerie and Cole want Ava's wedding to be as perfect as you do."

"You're right. Maybe I don't want to spend all my free time doing this, either."

She'd rather be fretting over the flowers, or the ice sculpture. Not a violet ribbon that should be blue. And God help her, she still had to talk to Dr. Long about jazz. She'd been about to take him aside last night, but then the dancing had started. And Geoff had showed up.

Maribel stood and picked up a box filled with favors. "Good thing you agreed, because I already asked Valerie for help. She's waiting for us."

"Maribel! You should have cleared this with me first."

"Why? I had *plans* to take a tour of the lighthouse today, spend some time at the beach. Plans you ruined."

"Fine." Jordan picked up three boxes. "You get the rest."

Maribel called Valerie to let her know the latest. Once they were on their way, Jordan finally relaxed. A little. She'd get help. Maybe that was the smart thing to do. She would need to learn to ask for help more often, just as Maribel suggested. It didn't mean she was weak or ineffective. Far from it. It took strength and overcoming foolish pride to admit one needed help.

"You know, part of the reason I *didn't* ask for help is because I thought maybe…maybe some people might think it's a bit anal retentive of me not to just go with the flow. A violet ribbon, or a blue ribbon. It wouldn't matter to *most* people."

Maribel leaned back in the passenger seat, eyes closed, a smile on her lips. "What matters is that everyone will realize this is about making the day perfect for Max and Ava. Whatever it takes."

Following the GPS in her rental, Jordan drove along the curvy coastline. Charming was a small, bucolic, picture-postcard coastal town with a quaint lighthouse, bridges, jetties and piers jutting out to the sea along the wharf. Today wasn't as oppressively hot as it had been on the day she'd arrived. In fact, a lovely light breeze carried through the air as they drove, windows rolled down.

"Wow," Maribel said when they pulled up. "Look at that. I've always wanted to see inside a lighthouse."

"Most of them are closed and not open to the public."

Jordan parked and took a moment to admire the regal fixture. The outside was a weather-beaten white with light blue trim. It had its own strip of private beach adjacent, where two Adirondack chairs sat in the sand. A surfboard stood propped up against the side.

Valerie, who must have heard them arrive, waited at the front door. "Hey, you two. Please come in."

When Valerie shut the door, Jordan stepped into a nautical world. Bright sunlight streamed through windows in streaks, leaving random patches of rays here and there. In the evening, Jordan imagined moonbeams doing more of the same. Windows gave her a breathtakingly beautiful view of the gulf. The teak wood floors gleamed.

"This is our home," Valerie said. "Kitchen, great room, guest bathroom that way. Upstairs, the bedrooms and a deck with an old-fashioned telescope."

Oh yes, the *stairs*. They were winding and led to a wraparound second-story landing with porthole windows. It was all…incredible.

Valerie smiled and pointed to the stairs where Jordan's gaze was riveted. "It's a recovered ship staircase."

"Dude, you're so lucky to live here," Maribel said, turning in a circle.

"Yes, that's what I tell myself every day. Even if it's going to be difficult to babyproof the place."

Jordan followed Valerie to the kitchen, where there were bowls of chips, pretzels, a plate of cookies, and bottles of water and soda.

"I thought we could get set up in here," Valerie said.

"You didn't have to do all this." Jordan felt guilty about the intrusion. "I wouldn't normally ask, but we're pressed for time. They got the order wrong."

"I'm happy to help. I've already taken maternity leave and I'm bored out of my mind. Cole won't let me waitress part-time anymore because my ankles were swollen after my last shift. Even if I was recently getting the best tips of my life." She patted her belly. "Everyone loves a baby and its hardworking mama."

Within minutes, they'd set up an assembly line, and after an hour, Jordan realized they might actually get these hammered out today.

Laughter filtered through the open windows and outside a dog barked.

"Sounds like the guys are back," Valerie said. "They went to get a little beach time with Susan."

Jordan froze in the middle of removing a violet ribbon. "You're babysitting Susan?"

"No. Rafe is here, too."

"Wait. Rafe is *here*?" Jordan narrowed her eyes at Maribel, who wouldn't look at Jordan. "Did you know this?"

Maribel shrugged.

"They're staying here with us. It was cheaper than renting a hotel room and we're happy to do it."

"Hey, ladies," Cole said, the first to walk through the open sliding glass doors.

Sub followed behind, then quickly found his dog bed in the adjacent living room and collapsed into it with a heavy sigh.

"Did y'all have fun?" Valerie asked, winding her arms around Cole's neck and kissing him.

"You can ask the man himself." Cole turned as Rafe ducked to walk inside, Susan high on his shoulders.

For a moment, Jordan's breath caught. She took in all the scenery at once. Rafe, relaxed and seemingly at ease in board shorts and…no shirt. His hair windblown and wild, he didn't appear as clean-cut as he'd been last night. Beard stubble dotted his jawline and chin. But it was his easy smile that made Jordan's stomach tighten.

"Hey," he said, meeting Jordan's gaze.

"Hi, Jordan!" Susan waved from the top of Rafe's broad shoulders.

"I didn't know you two were staying here." Jordan waved back. "How fun for Susan. A real lighthouse."

"And there's a tetascope upstairs!" Susan said. "Daddy, I want to show Jordan the tetascope."

"Telescope." Rafe set Susan down. "It looks like Jordan is busy."

"I'm sure I can take a few minutes," Jordan said,

setting down the blue ribbon she'd been about to hand to Maribel.

"Yay!" Susan ran to Jordan, took her hand and began to pull her up the staircase.

Chapter Thirteen

Rafe had been enjoying a relaxing beach day right up until the moment he walked inside and saw Jordan sitting at the table, the familiar boxes surrounding her. At least she was accepting some assistance. Her intractable stubbornness frustrated him.

He noted with interest that Jordan was here with Maribel. No *Geoff* in sight. But Rafe refused to get his hopes up because they'd left together last night. The man was probably holed up in her hotel room doing whatever lawyers did when they were outside of a courtroom. Probably lots of phone calls and scrolling. Last night, he'd caught the way he held Jordan's hand in one, and his cell in the other. Great multitasker. Rafe would give him that.

But the idiot didn't yet realize Jordan deserved

both of his hands. He'd certainly staked his claim when he'd introduced himself as Jordan's *fiancé*. Geoff and Jordan were together, and Rafe would respect that. Even if his gut churned with jealousy. No, make that envy. He had no *right* to be jealous.

"Look!" Susan pointed to the telescope when they reached the deck outside.

"This is what she wants to show you." He set his hand on the kind of telescope once used in an actual working lighthouse.

"Very cool."

"See? I told you!" Susan bounced up and down. She then climbed on the step stool Cole had set there so she could stand on her own.

"This is awesome," Jordan said, looking through the scope.

The scent of salt rose heavy in the air and seagulls squawked nearby. The Gulf Coast was gorgeous at this time of the year, but Rafe couldn't keep his eyes off Jordan. She stood with both hands on the rail of the deck, facing the ocean. Today she wore a simple short dress and sandals. She still had the best legs he'd ever seen in his life.

A seagull squawked and the wind whipped her hair into a frenzy of waves. Sometime in the past week she'd lost the straight look and was back to her wavy, wild hair. A welcome sight to him, though he doubted this was intentional on her part.

Jordan turned to Susan. "Ever see anything interesting out there?"

"Mermaids!" Susan squealed with delight. "But Daddy doesn't see them."

"Maybe Daddy just lacks imagination." Jordan met his eyes, and he didn't think he'd mistaken the flirty and teasing tone in her voice.

Only he might catch the nuance, but he knew her far too well to miss it.

He returned fire. "No, Daddy *doesn't* lack imagination. Shortie, give Jordan a turn." He picked Susan up and set her down, then beckoned to Jordan. "Here, see for yourself. Sometimes I can see cruise ships in the distance. And, at night, plenty of stars."

"I want another cookie!" Susan took off.

"Just one!" Rafe called out behind her, then turned to Jordan. "You want to take a look?"

He kicked the stool aside and Jordan moved in front of him. He stood directly behind her as she tilted the scope.

"This is where you adjust it." He moved close, positioned her hand and tried to ignore her sweet coconut scent.

He observed Jordan move the dial and look out on the vast gulf in the distance. From here they had a good view of the swelling waves as they rolled in from a distance and crashed on the rocks below.

"Have *you* ever seen anything interesting?"

"A dolphin. The waters are too warm, and Cole said that's a rarity. A good omen."

"You didn't see a mermaid? Now, *that* would have been a good sign."

"My imagination lies in other areas. I don't see fabled sea creatures like my daughter does." He barely resisted the urge to touch her, even to simply put his hand low on her back.

She turned to him suddenly and they were closer than he'd realized as she faced him. He wasn't quite noble enough to take a step back. So she did.

"I guess there's no almost-engagement anymore, is there? Congratulations are in order. Where's your fiancé today?"

"I sent Geoff home." She met his eyes. "We broke up."

This was the best development he'd heard of in years. He quickly corrected himself because he should have sympathy for Jordan. Even if the same teeth-gnashing and bone-melting pain of their breakup wasn't in her eyes. Breakups were tough. She might be disguising her feelings in front of him, for many reasons, not the least of them being pride.

"Well, I guess...I should say I'm sorry."

After all, he knew better than anyone else what it was like to lose Jordan.

"I didn't break up with him because you showed up to the wedding, all handsome and flirty. I didn't do it for *you*."

Even better news. *She* broke up with Geoff. But okay, *not* for Rafe. He wouldn't have expected that anyway. One of the things he'd loved most about Jordan was her loyalty. She didn't give up on people easily. She hadn't arrived at this decision overnight. It had probably been niggling at her for months.

"Why did you?"

"For me." She turned away from him again, turning the scope to look elsewhere. "I'm going to be alone for a while and see what that feels like for a change."

"That's pretty much where I am right now."

Okay, so this wasn't 100 percent true. Just the other night he was willing to engage in a little uncomplicated sex with Becca. He still believed this phenom to be a rare unicorn, but hope sprang eternal in the heart of a single father with not much time on his hands.

She snorted. "That's funny. You didn't look too lonely the other night with Becca."

When the wind blew hair over her eye, he reached to push it out of her way the moment she did, and their fingers collided.

"You already know it didn't go well." He cleared his throat. "Turns out, I never learned how to date."

"Interesting. You seemed to be doing fine."

Was that a hint of irritation he heard in her voice? He was well acquainted with that lilt of frustration and jealousy in her tone. Quite familiar, unfortunately.

"Then I must fake it well. I had no idea what I was doing. I've never dated much."

"What do you mean? We used to date. For *years*."

"I'm not sure you could call it that. We were in a relationship."

She cocked her head. "Which started with a *date*."

"One." He shrugged. "All I remember is asking you if you wanted to go to the movies with me, Max and a bunch of our other friends. I held your hand and stole a kiss when no one was looking. Next thing you know, bam! I was in love."

She smiled and a moment passed between them, thick and raw with memories.

She shook her head and pointed between them. "That was then, this is now. You and me, we're... impossible."

"I wouldn't say *impossible*. Anything is possible."

"Unlikely, then. You and Liz, take two, now that's entirely possible. Even likely."

He met her eyes. "No, Jordan. Not going to happen."

"How can you be so sure?"

"Because I don't love her other than as a good friend and my daughter's mother." He waited a beat, wondering if he could bring up such a sensitive issue right now, when things were going so well between them. "Jordan, I never cheated on you. Never. If you think about it, you'll know it's true. You were the one to first give up on us."

Jordan simply stared back at him, and for an interminable second, neither one of them said a word.

"Daddy, Daddy, Daddy!" Susan bounded up the

steps, Sub right behind her. "I taught Sub a new trick."

"Excuse me." Jordan brushed by him on her way downstairs.

Jordan rushed down the spiral staircase. She was having trouble taking in a deep breath as memories rushed back. There wasn't time for these thoughts but thanks to Rafe, they were again taking up residence.

The few times Jordan had met Liz and Travis Kelly were on their short trips to California. Instead of it being a double date with two couples, however, Jordan had felt like the outsider when the fellow soldiers commiserated. They talked about future deployments and the "sandbox." Liz was one of the guys, who cursed with the best of them, loud, strong and confident. She had short blond hair and wore the look better than any woman Jordan had ever seen. They were a trio more than they were a quartet. When Jordan thought Liz's gazes lingered a little too long and salaciously toward Rafe, she simply excused it, because she didn't understand their world. Crude jokes were common and sexual innuendos the norm.

Rafe turned this way down for Jordan, as did Max, but Travis and Liz were a different story. Travis spoke some of the saltiest humor Jordan had ever heard and joked he'd been lucky to meet Liz first, because she'd always wanted a *Latin* lover.

"Watch out for her," Maribel warned. "She's tough and she takes what she wants. And she wants *Rafe*."

Jordan's insecurities had eventually gotten the better of her. All the trips Rafe would take to Atlanta to "check in" on Liz and Travis. Maribel's words ringing in Jordan's ears: *watch out for her.*

"Are you having an affair with Liz?"

He'd given her a look like she'd lost leave of her senses. "Are you out of your mind? She's madly in love with Travis, who's one of my best friends."

"But *are* you?"

"Hell, no."

But what would he say: *yes, you caught me*? Their fights grew uglier, and epic, as Jordan let loose with her greatest fears. Every time he came home, he was less himself. He didn't love her anymore because, wait for it...

She didn't belong anymore.

She wasn't part of Rafe's inner circle.

He'd changed.

And before Rafe could break up with her, she'd beaten him there.

"You don't mean it. You're just mad. Look, I'm going now, so you can cool down. And I'll call you tomorrow."

Rafe attended the field training he often had between his deployments and they were separated once more. Angry and frustrated, she'd ignored Rafe's frequent emails, text messages, calls and attempts to reconcile.

Even Max had tried to intervene.

No, I meant it, Max. Stop getting in the middle of this. Rafe and I broke up. Let him stew a while. See how much he misses me. I've always made it too easy for him.

She'd even asked for advice from her mother, who, in her old-school way, claimed Jordan should continue to play "hard to get." She'd even gone on a date or two, which never went anywhere. But six weeks later, as she set up the wooden fruit stand where her family occasionally sold strawberries on weekends, she saw the letters Rafe had etched into the wood in a place where no one else could see:

R loves J ~ forever

And she couldn't stay away from him any longer. She would never love anyone else or be with anyone else. It had to be Rafe. Rafe, who was the love of her life.

Jordan's jealousy had obviously colored her view, not at all helped by Maribel's warnings.

I'm sorry we fought, she'd finally texted Rafe back. I love you, too. Forever.

But that, as it turned out, was a text sent too late.

Chapter Fourteen

Maribel met Jordan at the bottom of the stairs. "Cole is making margaritas!"

The blender roared, and country music played lightly in the background, the mood light. The atmosphere had turned jovial and celebratory, appropriate for wedding week.

Jordan pulled herself back from the fruit stand in Watsonville where Rafe had told her, after Travis's death, that he'd be marrying Liz and moving to Atlanta to help raise Susan.

But Maribel sensed the mood shift immediately. "What's wrong?"

Jordan, I never cheated on you. Never.

"Nothing."

This was sister code for *I'll tell you later.*

Maribel nodded and handed over Jordan's cell. "Your phone has been pinging off the hook."

"Thanks."

Great. A distraction. Work had always managed to give her a healthy outlet. Workaholic or not, she needed something *else* to think about. The call was from the local florist and Jordan stepped outside to return it.

"I was just getting ready to call and confirm our order again. How are those flowers coming along?"

"I'm sorry about this," the woman on the other end of the line said.

"S-sorry? About what?" Fear spread like tentacles. This did not sound good. No one should be sorry for *anything* this close to a wedding day.

"We've had to cancel the order. The staff is down due to the stomach flu."

"The entire *store*?"

"Everyone. I don't actually work here. The shop belongs to my parents. I'm just here making phone calls and helping where I can."

Oh no, this could not be happening. *Not now.*

"D-do you know anything about floral arrangements?"

"Don't worry, my parents are going to be okay," the girl said, heavy on the sarcasm.

Jordan cringed. Sometimes when she got wrapped in her work, she forgot other people's feelings. She'd been raised better.

"I'm so sorry. I should have asked about them first. I'm glad they'll be okay."

"Thank you. Ta-da! I have a florist for y'all."

"Whew! Why didn't you say so?"

"We tried to get one closer, but this *is* the start of wedding season. Everyone is booked. Anyway, they're a bit of a distance, over in San Antonio, but Posey Rosey Florists said they can squeeze the order in. Unfortunately, they're not going to be able to deliver them to you. You'll have to go pick them up."

"No problem. San Antonio? How far is that? Is that anywhere near Houston?"

She laughed. "You must not be from Texas. No, it's Hill Country. They do beautiful work. Believe me, you'll be happy."

Hill Country? Jordan didn't know much about Texas geography, but that sounded *far*.

"So you'll have to pick them up, and I'd do it soon, just to be safe."

Sailing straight into panic mode was making Jordan a little dizzy and lightheaded. "Give me the address, and whatever you do, *do not* call the bride."

"Sorry, I already did. She sounded like she was crying. Pretty dramatic, actually. You'd think I told her somebody died. But she got it together enough to give me your phone number."

Oh, for the love of brides! Could this day *get* any worse?

As Jordan paced the beach, no longer finding the sounds of seagulls quite as enchanting, she phoned

Ava. In the background, she heard music and the sounds of footsteps.

Jordan spoke loudly. "I don't want you to even break a sweat, honey. This is what I do. I'm going to get those flowers if I have to rent a plane to get them here."

"Are you sure? I *guess* we can have a wedding without flowers…"

"Absolutely not! You, of all people, need flowers. We can't let one little stomach flu get us down. This is why you have me."

"Max," Ava sniffled off the phone. "Jordan says it's going to be all right."

"I *told* you my sister would take care of this. Hang up the phone, baby. C'mere."

Jordan's heart swelled at the faith Max had in her. When she stepped back inside, Cole was pouring from the blender. Rafe and Susan were dancing to "We Don't Talk About Bruno," Maribel was sipping from her blended drink and Valerie was using the glue gun.

Jordan, I never cheated on you. Never. God, it was true. She believed him. *Finally.* About four years too late.

It was Rafe who noticed Jordan first and shut the music off. "What's wrong?"

"There's a problem with the flowers. How far is San Antonio from here?"

"About three hours. Why?" Cole said.

After she finished explaining the dilemma, she

realized she had another problem: a vehicle large enough to accommodate the flowers.

"The good news is we're done with the wedding favors." Valerie held up a beautiful silver and *blue* ribboned box.

"Thank you!" Then, flying into chief organizer and event planner mode, Jordan turned and scanned the room.

"Now, does anyone have a truck or van I can borrow?"

A few minutes and several discussions later, it was eventually decided by a consensus that Rafe should be the one to drive Jordan to San Antonio because *he* had the van. Valerie and Cole would watch Susan, Maribel said she would stay to help out and drive Jordan's rental back to the hotel. If reinforcements were needed, they'd call Adam and Stacy. Everyone agreed, after Jordan nearly threatened them, that Max and Ava should not, under *any* circumstances, be bothered.

With a three-hour drive each way, they would return late tonight. Rafe had campaigned for an early morning start tomorrow, but that would make the timeline too close to the wedding and Jordan refused. Anything could happen. On this, he was forced to agree.

Finally, they were on their way, Jordan sitting in the front passenger seat. "Why did you rent a van?"

"When I got to the car rental place, all they had left

was this van, and a snazzy little sports car. I would have loved *that* car, but the van is safer."

"And your middle-aged crisis is still a few years away. The sports car can wait."

"Funny. It came in handy the other night at the rehearsal dinner where I was the designated driver." He paused for a beat. "Do I at least get points for being a good dad?"

"Yes, but right now, that's *all* you get points for."

"Fair enough. Have you ever had to do anything like this before? Pick up flowers in another city to save the day?" He was trying to make idle conversation, and of course, he was terrible at it.

"Never."

"How horrible would it be *not* to have flowers?"

She turned to give him a horrified look, as if she'd come up on the devil himself. "If you don't want to come with me, *I* can drive the van. I don't need you."

"You do need me."

"Not if you're going to complain and wonder out loud why a wedding needs *flowers*. Suppose I asked you whether this van needs gasoline. How would you answer that question?"

"Okay, thank you for putting it into terms I understand. Flowers are to a wedding what gasoline is to a vehicle."

"A *wedding* is a special time for two people who are in love and planning to pledge their lives to each other. It's not time to cut corners. This one day sets the tone for the rest of their lives."

"Or not."

He eased on to the highway, intent on making conversation. And even if the topic was dangerous to them, he went ahead.

"It seems what's most important is the marriage itself."

"I'm not a therapist. By the time couples get to this point, I'm going to assume they know what's important and what's not. You can probably agree with me on at least one thing. Ava and Max have what it takes for a successful marriage."

"Absolutely. Those two are going to be fine. Whether they have flowers or not."

"Oh, they're *going* to have flowers."

"Of course, they are. Because we're driving to San Antonio to get them."

"I would hire a chartered plane if that's what it took." She fiddled with the radio dial and pushed buttons until she found a station playing country music. Then she turned it up.

He got the message: *Shut up, Rafe.*

She was pissy now, and even in his addled state, he understood it couldn't be all about the flowers. It was him, bringing up an old and tired subject. They drove quietly for the first hour while he wondered if her irritation was truly with him or the situation. By now she should realize that life happened, and people rolled with the punches.

She was working without her planner, with botched wedding favors and now a problem with the flowers. Surely he wasn't the only one in this vehicle who understood the concept? Newsflash: life didn't always turn out the way one had planned.

He was exhibit A, driving exhibit B. "Just tell me one thing."

"All right."

"Do you finally believe I was faithful to you?" He didn't have to give her any more details.

She bristled and moved in her seat. "Maybe I do, but can you see how that would have been difficult to accept, especially after what happened?"

"Yes." He shook his head. "But you know me. You had to know it wasn't true."

"By then, it didn't matter, did it? You got *married*."

"All that matters now is that you believe me. I was devastated after you ended it. By the time you changed your mind about us, it was too late."

"I was there, Rafe. I know."

A silence passed between them, long, uncomfortable and thick with regret on his part.

"Want to stop for lunch?" he asked several minutes later.

"We don't have time."

"All right, if you're hungry, just whistle."

But over an hour into the silence, Rafe noticed a massive slowdown ahead of them. The kind of traffic that, to him, meant EMS would likely be on their way, if not already there.

"What's happening?" Jordan sat up straighter, looking in front, and then behind them.

"Could be an accident."

"I hope no one is badly hurt."

"Unfortunately, the odds of no injuries in an accident on the highway are not great."

"How would you know?"

"I work as a first responder in Dallas. Paramedic."

"I didn't know that. I guess there's a lot I don't know about you anymore."

"Because you haven't bothered to ask. And I'm insulted that you haven't stalked me on social media."

"Sorry, I stopped stalking after the happy photo Liz posted of your family."

"I wasn't *happy*."

"You looked happy."

He grunted and went back to the original and safer subject.

"Turns out a paramedic just might be the worst career for a father. Last month, I transported three teenagers to the hospital with severe injuries from an MVA. They'd been texting and driving."

"Oh my God. I do that sometimes."

"Not anymore you don't."

"It's not like I make a habit out of it, *Rafe*."

"See that you don't." He quirked a brow. "Susan isn't going to drive until she's thirty years old."

"Oh, well, *that's* realistic."

"And she'll *never* own a cell phone, if I have anything to do with it."

She snorted. "Dreamer."

The traffic slowed to a complete stop and Rafe

wondered if they'd closed the highway. Accidents large enough to completely close a major highway were rare. He didn't want to share this bit of information with Jordan. Not yet.

"Are we stopping? On the *freeway*?"

"Yeah."

"Oh, Lord. This is bad, isn't it?"

"Let's not get ahead of ourselves." He shut off the engine. "I'll be right back."

The moment he opened the door, he was assaulted by the smell of smoke, thick in the air. Just ahead, skies were dark gray, nearly black in spots. Texas had been plagued by crazy spring storms, tornadoes and brush fires this year. He walked several yards up the fire lane, and judging by the display ahead, they could be here for a while.

"What did you find out?" Jordan asked when he returned.

"Lots of smoke in the air and up ahead it could be worse. Might be another out-of-control brush fire. This time of the year, high winds and heat make a perfect storm." He turned the radio dial to a local station broadcast, hoping for news updates.

Jordan pulled out her phone and started swiping. "I can't believe this. What else could go wrong?"

"Don't even ask that."

A hell of a lot more could go wrong and he fought against the tide of memories.

"Face it, she's done with you, Rafe." Liz had handed him back his cell after reading Jordan's text message.

"There must be something I can do to get her back. She's never ignored me like this before."

But nothing had worked. Not his frequent texts, emails or phone calls professing his love. She ignored him, and a sense of doom enveloped him. He'd lost her for good. Even with frequent absences due to his deployments, they'd always come back to each other. But the loss of Travis had destroyed more than one man.

Liz had been a comfort to Rafe when he too felt he'd lost everything that ever mattered to him.

"We've both lost the loves of our lives."

Liz suggested marriage, and he'd impulsively agreed, wanting the golf ball of pain to finally slide down his throat so he could breathe again. Reaching for any happiness he could find. But he didn't love Liz. He loved Susan and that was supposed to be enough.

Stupid.

Eventually, vehicles began to slowly move again. And after another mile the source of the issue became clear. Several fire trucks and EMS personnel had blocked the freeway, and all cars were being redirected to one single lane.

Rafe turned to Jordan. "We're being forced off the highway."

Forced off the highway.

In all her years of weddings, Jordan had never had this many challenges thrown at her all at once. First, a wedding where Rafe would be the best man.

She'd accepted that as inevitable. Max had been kind enough to ask her if she'd have a tough time with it, and she'd professed to be completely over Rafe. And she had been, or so she thought.

Next, a flower shop had come down with the flu. The entire *store*. The only replacement florist available was three hours away. Each way.

Rafe. A self-explanatory complication. He *had* to be the only one with a vehicle large enough to bring the flowers.

Lastly, this highway disaster. A brush fire or some such thing. She didn't want to know what else could go wrong. What if they'd come too early for the flowers, and they'd be wilted by the time of the wedding? What if they didn't get to San Antonio in time and they closed the shop? What if, what if, what if. Her brain began to plot reactions for each scenario.

Police had directed traffic to an exit and the line of cars snaked through at the rate of approximately one per hour by her calculations. The GPS on the rental said they were all being dumped in Gonzalez, which, according to Google Maps, was still not *anywhere* near San Antonio.

This was not part of the plan. And seriously, how could anyone anticipate any of this? Of course, Texas had fires. But how often did a highway get closed for one? Insurance companies would call this an "act of God" and probably deny coverage.

Beside her, Rafe continued to appear as if a *hurricane* wouldn't faze him. She would appreciate if he would join her in this panic-fest she was enduring all alone.

"*How* can you be so calm?"

He scowled. "Who the hell said I'm calm?"

"Your face!"

Meanwhile, she was ready to go back to her childhood habit of biting her nails till they bled. This delay would cost them hours, no doubt. They'd be back after midnight now, if they even made it to San Antonio before the shop closed. In that case, it would make more sense to simply stay the night and wait until morning. Which was when Rafe had wanted to leave.

Meanwhile, they were in a small town where they'd be lucky to find lunch.

"Don't worry, Zippy. I've got you."

He reached for her hand, squeezed it, and damn if she didn't feel a thrum of relief roll through her. She had *Rafe*. Before…everything, he'd always been there for her. He would get her through this. He'd find a way to get them to San Antonio.

She could relax for a minute. Unwind. Trust someone else for a change. It had been such a long time since she'd trusted Rafe. But he'd proved he wanted to help, going over and beyond with the wedding favors. Searching for her lost planner.

Jordan, I never cheated on you. Never.

She studied his profile, the set jaw that could cut glass, his sharp features.

"Yes. Yes, okay, you have my back. I believe you."

He quirked a brow. "I'm honored."

"Don't make me *sorry* I said it."

"I guess we have time for lunch." He reached behind his seat. "Almost forgot. Here you go."

He set a wrapped box on her lap. "What's this?"

"A new one."

The package was beautifully wrapped in silver and *blue* paper.

"I didn't wrap it." Rafe cleared his throat. "Got it at the bookstore."

"Blue and silver?"

"Yeah, I *did* ask for that. Private joke."

She tore open the wrapping paper to find a brand-new planner. "Oh, Rafe. This…is so kind. Thank you for this."

"It's not as nice as the one you had but until you replace it…"

The book was actually fancier than the one she'd had. Leather bound, with white tooling on the cover. He really was trying, and she could try to be nicer. More forgiving.

He'd searched for her lost planner in the dumpster. And as if that wasn't enough, he'd gifted her with a better one.

"I've been writing on slips of paper and leaving them all over the place."

She flipped through the pages, admiring the layout. On page two, Rafe had listed his address in Dallas, his phone number, place of business and favorite restaurants in the area. He'd even listed Susan's pre-school and his weekend visitation schedule.

The nature of those words said something deeply personal to her. They meant more than "I'm sorry." They meant more than "please forgive me."

They meant: *"don't forget me."*

"Hope you don't mind, but I wrote in it first."

She didn't mind at all. In fact, her heart squeezed at the obvious desire to keep in touch.

They wound their way through the two-stoplight town, and Rafe pulled over at a gas station. He searched maps on the GPS.

"I'm going to review our options."

"I'll get us something to drink."

Emerging from the van, she coughed at the thick, smoky smell in the air. This was a bad one. She'd never been this close to the action but had friends in the Sonoma area who'd had to evacuate their homes during California's last wildfire season.

The gas station had a shop inside and Jordan picked up a couple of cold sodas and a big bag of chips.

Goodbye, healthy eating. I'm going to indulge in a little stress eating today if you don't mind.

She and Rafe weren't the only ones who'd stopped, and a line formed behind Jordan.

"The highway may be closed for the rest of the day, or at least until they get the brush fire ninety percent controlled," a customer said. "There's a lot of debris blown all over the highway."

"This wind is insane. My app says the fire is only ten percent contained," said another, holding up his phone.

"We're not far from home, honey. We'll just take the back roads," a man could be heard telling his female companion.

"Lucky you," said the customer in front of Jordan. "We were on our way to San Antonio."

"Good luck," said the salesclerk. "The back roads might take an extra day and you might find trouble there, too. May as well wait it out."

By the time she got back to the van, Jordan was ready for Rafe's bad news. "What's the plan?"

"I'd like a little more time to review our options, but I suggest we try to book hotel rooms for the night. By morning this probably won't be an issue."

"Okay, you were right. We should have waited until morning. Are you happy?"

"No," he said from under lowered lashes. "Not happy."

"What about Susan? Won't she be upset to find you're not there in the morning?"

"She'll be easily distracted by Sub and the telescope."

"Don't make yourself sound so dispensable."

"I didn't mean to, but don't forget I'm a part-time father. We've spent plenty of nights apart. She's the child of divorce and understands better than you realize."

The words fell like sharp rocks. It wasn't her fault Liz and Rafe divorced, so why did she feel like it was?

"My other suggestion is we go find a restaurant and wait this out. But there are no guarantees the road will be open by tonight. There's apparently a lot of debris these winds have blown through that has to be cleared off the highway first."

Yes, she'd heard. Jordan swallowed. She did not want to be stuck spending the night anywhere near Rafe. Too tempting to forget everything between them just for one night.

No one would have to know. Not Max. Not Ava. Certainly not her parents. Just once for old times' sake. A fling.

Maribel, get out of my head!

"Okay, okay. Let's go get something to eat."

Chapter Fifteen

There were two establishments in town. The Mexican restaurant was filled, harboring at least some current refugees of the Highway 10 closure. When the first restaurant had a two-hour wait to be seated, they drove to the second one, and waited an hour.

"I'm going to order the juiciest cheeseburger they have," Rafe said, viewing the menu. "French fries, Coca-Cola and a banana split sundae."

"Good grief, where do you put it all?"

She viewed the menu, torn between the choice between the healthy meal and getting what she wanted. A plain burger and crunchy warm fries.

"Order whatever you want. It's on me."

She snapped her menu shut. "I think I'll splurge tonight and join you in the heart attack special."

"Anything you want."

Not *anything* she wanted. She couldn't rewind time and get back the last few years, knowing Rafe had been stuck in an unhappy marriage. She'd broken up with Geoff when it had become clear she didn't love him enough. But she couldn't imagine marrying anyone while being in love with someone else. Yet that had been Rafe. Missing her when he was married to Liz. Maribel had been right about one thing: Liz had gotten what she wanted. What she probably hadn't expected was that Jordan would make it easy.

The waitress came and took their orders and Jordan busied herself by checking out the decor in this greasy spoon diner. Early Americana, clearly. The booths were classic vinyl red, ripped in places, complete with well-worn Formica tables. She was surprised they didn't have a jukebox in the corner.

"Will you answer a question for me?" Rafe spoke, forcing her to look at him.

Bad idea. She went back to staring at the decor. Not at Rafe, his beard stubble and windblown hair giving him the air of a devilish rogue. When everyone decided earlier that he would drive Jordan, he'd changed from his board shorts into dark jeans and still wore the same black T-shirt. It seemed possibly a size too small, which was beginning to irritate her. She didn't want to notice these things. Things like Rafe's taut muscles and the ripped physique of a man who didn't spend a lot of time on the couch. Or at his desk.

"Go ahead. Ask. It's not like we're going anywhere."

"Are you and Geoff done for good?"

This was the last question she thought he'd ask her. "Yes. We are."

"No chance of reconciliation?"

Since that was pretty much what she'd suggested to him about Liz, she had it coming. It was an intrusive, personal question, but on the other hand, this was *Rafe*. She'd allow it.

"Like I said, I need to be on my own for a while. No. There's no chance."

"Do you love him?"

"I thought I did." She pierced him with the glare she'd perfected when dealing with caterers who arrived late. "I thought he loved me, too, but it obviously wasn't enough to marry me. Maybe I just never wanted to wind up alone."

"You wouldn't be the first couple who married for that reason. Maybe you had common goals, a similar vision."

She ignored the correlation he'd made to his own torpedoed marriage and her failed engagement. He would get absolutely no sympathy from her. Yes, she'd almost allowed herself to believe that shared goals for a financially stable future were enough for a solid marriage. Even joining together to raise a precious child wasn't always enough.

"Maybe my standards are higher."

She fiddled with the salt and pepper shakers, arranging them in a more orderly manner. The catsup, too, and sugar packets. The real sugar mixed with the Stevia. What a hot mess.

Rafe watched her, a hint of amusement in his eyes. A smile quirked at his lips. "You can't help yourself, can you?"

"What do you mean?"

"Everything has to be in perfect order, or you freak out." He took the saltshaker and slid it to his side of the table.

"What are you doing?"

"Freaking you out." The hint of a smile turned into a wicked one.

"Now you're being childish."

But she reached for the salt and tried to wrestle it back from him, wondering why only Rafe made her behave like a twelve-year-old again. He wouldn't let it go, either, and they continued to fight over a damn saltshaker.

"Let *go*," she said.

"*You* let go." His warm hand covered hers.

She struggled, slapping him away with one hand, then covering his hand with hers. "It belongs next to the pepper shaker. What is *wrong* with you?"

"Maybe my standards are higher. I'm trying something new with the saltshaker."

Neither one of them was going to let go, which meant Jordan was indeed a very different person than the girl Rafe had once loved.

At one time, she would have given in, made it a joke, because she was all about Rafe. Pleasing him.

Being there for him. Supporting him and his military career. Supporting him, period. Her friends were his friends. His friends were her friends.

Except when they weren't.

The waitress arrived with their plates. "Y'all want another saltshaker?"

The interruption made Jordan let go and then so did Rafe.

Jordan cleared her throat and pulled her hands back on her lap. "No. That's...that's fine."

"We're good." Rafe winked at the waitress.

She then nearly fell over herself making sure Rafe had everything he needed for the complicated meal of a cheeseburger and French fries.

"Would you like mayonnaise with your burger?" she asked. "Mustard? Mushrooms? The cook makes some awesome sautéed onions."

"No, thanks."

"Catsup?" she asked.

With a smile, Jordan held up the bottle sitting on the table next to the salt and pepper shakers and handed it over to Rafe.

"Oh, yeah." The waitress giggled. "Y'all let me know if you need anything else."

When she finally left, Jordan rolled her eyes. "Wink at her again and she'll have your children."

He grinned. "Not interested."

"In more children, or a relationship?"

"Both would be nice someday. I would like to have another child. One of my own."

"Susan *is* your own."

"I like to think so, but it isn't easy. Liz never lets me forget who's the real parent. I should have adopted her when I had the chance but at the time that felt like an insult to Kelly. I always wanted her to know her real father and what a great man he was."

"Rafe, you are her real father."

"I'm her father here on earth and she has another one in heaven."

"Does she already know what happened to Travis?"

"She doesn't fully understand, which is the way I like it. I figure I'll explain more when she gets older." Rafe cleared his throat. "Since he never actually… got to meet her."

The words fell between them, stilling the air. Then the entrance door chimed with the arrival of more customers and the silence broke.

"If marrying Liz was for the sake of Susan, then what you did was very kind. Honorable. Very…you."

"I admit at the time it felt like a sacrifice. Like I'd have to give up everything I ever loved for Susan's sake." He slid her a significant look. "Now it feels like I won the lottery. I get to be the father of this amazing little girl."

"And she gets to have you for a dad."

They ate quietly for several minutes, forgetting the past few minutes of idiocy. She didn't know how or why order had become so important in her life. Even *she* hadn't realized it would extend to *saltshak-*

ers. She would examine this in the future, but for now blame it on current stress levels. Lately, she'd felt herself slowly unraveling like a spool of yarn.

After they'd finished eating, Rafe took out his phone. "The road is still closed. Estimates of reopening are all over the place. The soonest is two in the morning."

Jordan moaned, closed her eyes and pressed fingers to her temples. She no longer saw any other way.

"Okay, fine. Let's get a couple of rooms for the night. I'll let the flower shop know we'll be there in the morning."

Rafe didn't want to say "I told you so" *out loud,* but the first hotel was booked by the time they arrived. Not even one room available.

They had better luck at the second hotel. "Great news!" the desk clerk said. "We have one room left."

"One?" Jordan squeaked from next to him.

"I'm sorry, but the freeway closure has us fully booked, a rarity. You understand."

Rafe nodded. "Yes, *we* do."

Resisting the urge to tell Jordan she should have listened to him in the first place when he wanted to book a hotel room, he pulled out his wallet.

"We'll take it."

Rafe signed all the paperwork and the clerk handed over two card keys. He led the way to the first-floor room, which happened to be at the end of the hallway near the snack dispensers and ice machine. The machine hummed loudly right next to their room.

"Lovely place," he muttered and swiped the card.

Inside were two double beds, which meant he wouldn't have to sleep on the floor. Fortunately, though the room gave new meaning to "economy," everything appeared to be sanitized and clean.

Jordan had called the florist, but Rafe hadn't talked to Susan yet. He pulled out his phone, dialed Cole and explained the situation.

"Daddy? Why aren't you *here*?" Susan asked.

"There's a problem with the road. It's closed and we can't get through."

"Then come back."

"I can't come back until tomorrow, Shortie. We still have to pick up the flowers."

"But why?"

Rafe closed his eyes and pinched the bridge of his nose. Not *this*. He was too tired, too spent, too sexually frustrated to play twenty questions.

"Because a wedding needs special flowers. My friend Max needs these flowers for his wedding, or he'll be very unhappy."

"But why?"

"Because my friend Jordan said so."

Susan seemed stumped for a second, but then a moment later, "But why?"

He briefly considered pretending to lose the connection. "Hey, how about if I read you a bedtime story?"

"Over the phone again?"

Before Liz agreed to share custody with Rafe, she'd kept Susan away for two months while she considered her options and spoken with an attorney. During that time, he'd talked to her every night and often read her to sleep.

"Why not? It will be fun. It's been a while since we did that."

"Okay, Daddy. I'm ready. And I want the one about the beautiful princess who married her prince. And then a bad man came and turned him into a toad. And then…"

"Am I telling the story, or are you?"

The fairy tale he'd spun together in those first few weeks of separation was sort of a memoir. Except unlike the fictional telling, Rafe had turned *himself* into a toad, but hey, it turned out writing fiction wasn't easy. In the end, he'd given himself the happily-ever-after he'd wanted.

Realizing Jordan was quietly listening from the chair next to him, he spun the tale of the beautiful princess with a large and happy family. She and her brother welcomed the pauper into their family, and they all became best friends. Eventually, the princess married the pauper. He became her prince. But then along came an evil wizard who turned the prince into a toad. He hopped along the forest asking for help from everyone in finding his way back to the princess and breaking the spell.

"Good night, honey. Always remember you're my special princess."

"Tell her I said good night," Jordan said.

Rafe did, and after approximately one hundred more good-nights, he hung up. It might seem odd to some parents, but he was used to being separated from his daughter for long periods of time. Sad but true.

When he glanced in Jordan's direction, she was studying him, probably catching the hints of his own history in the fairy tale.

Toad, meet your lost princess.

"You're a wonderful father," Jordan said. "And I'm not at all surprised."

Rafe only understood what it had been like for him, growing up without one. A single mother, who did the best she could. He'd learned only one thing: how *not* to be a father.

Don't yell at your kid. Don't yell at their mother. Don't leave them.

"I try."

He emptied his jean pockets of keys and wallet and tossed them on the dresser, with no idea of how to behave in this situation. If this was a hotel with an actual lobby, he might excuse himself and give her some alone time. But other than taking a walk outside and breathing in the lovely stench of brush fire smoke, he didn't see any options. They were kind of stuck together for now.

"I'll take this one." Jordan sat on one bed and smoothed down the covers.

"Next to the *door*? I should take that bed in case something happens. You take the other one."

She made a face. "I'm not afraid of the boogeyman and I don't need your protection. This bed is fine."

"And how did *you* get to decide?"

While his actions in the past few hours were making him realize he spent too much time around a four-year-old, it was a valid question.

"You want to flip a coin?" She crossed her arms and studied him from under lowered eyelashes.

"That would be fair."

"Really. You're being childish again."

"We wouldn't even be in this position if not for you. I did what you asked and waited to book a hotel room. *Big* mistake."

"Well, I'm sorry. I didn't want you to leave Susan alone all night. Now you won't be there when she wakes up in the morning. How could I know the highway would be shut down overnight?"

"Why didn't you let me book a hotel room just in case?"

She snorted. "*Let* you? That implies I have any control over what you do."

"Of course you have control!" His voice rose in volume. "Why the hell am I driving to San Antonio if not for you?"

She quirked a brow. "You had a choice to stay behind."

"I did *not* have a choice. The van is insured to me and I'm not going to let you drive all this way alone."

"Well, excuse me for dragging you along. I know what that's like." She crossed her arms.

"What's that supposed to mean?"

"It means when we were together, I was simply along for the ride. Well, no more, buddy." She shook a finger. "And you can't stand it. I have my own mind and my own plans."

"I have no idea where this is coming from. How were you along for the ride?"

"Don't pretend you don't know. You had a duty and honor to the military before anyone and anything else. And I had to fall in line, too."

"You knew that about me. It's what I signed up for. And so did Max."

"Well, I didn't sign up for it. And excuse me if I had no way of knowing your *service* would include marrying the wife of a fallen soldier. Really, that goes beyond the pale."

"Good, let's talk about this. Air it out. We should."

"No, we're *not* talking about it! I refuse to discuss this with you." She rose, pointed at him and began to pace the room.

"Fine, I'll talk, and you listen."

He would choose his words carefully and hope they would make her snap and get it all out of her system. Right now, he was about as far from control as a man could get. All semblance of civility slipped away and slid through his fingers like grains of sand. He was so tired of apologizing and groveling for a decision he'd made with the best of intentions.

The road to hell... Yeah, genius, preach it. You learned the hard way.

Jordan turned on him, her eyes flashing with anger. "You both made a mockery out of marriage.

You pretended you could take the *place* of Travis Kelly."

"Jordan—"

"Do you know what it's like to love someone who puts obligation to someone *else* first? What it's like when they have a greater loyalty to something else? Yours was to the military, then to Travis, then to Liz and Susan. I always came last. And I'll never forgive you for that!"

The words hit him like stray bullets, and one hit a major artery. She was right, of course. They weren't a casualty of war like Travis Kelly had been. He and Jordan had become a casualty of peacetime negotiations.

But even with all this mature knowledge, from somewhere deep inside, anger snaked through him.

"The problem is *you* don't understand what it's like to have a duty and commitment to something greater than yourself."

"How dare you."

The words had sliced at the desired nerve. She reached him in two swift steps and slapped his cheek. Her hand hung in the air between them, her eyes filled with a chaos of warring emotions. It took only a second for the hot charge of anger in her dark eyes to move swiftly to shock, and then a look he recognized as regret. Watery eyes gazed into his with confusion. Her lower lip trembled, and she bit into it, looking away.

He reached for the hand she'd slapped him with

and brought it to his lips. Kissed it, then rolled it over and kissed her palm.

"Rafe," she said. "I'm s-sorry."

"Don't be. I clearly deserved that."

"No, you *didn't*."

"I pushed you, and for that, I'm the one who's sorry." He didn't let go of her hand, threading her fingers through his own. "But this had to happen. You've been waiting to hit me for years."

"No." She shook her head. "It's…complicated."

"I never cheated on you, Jordan. Never."

"You've already said that. But do you understand how hard that was to believe?"

"I do. I thought you and I were really done. And then Liz proposed because we'd both lost so much, that we try to make a marriage work. For Susan's sake."

Rafe hadn't ever made a choice between Jordan and Liz. He'd chosen between Jordan and *Susan*. Most fathers didn't have to choose between the woman they loved and the child they adored. Both deserved equal protection. Respect.

But unfortunately, he wasn't most fathers.

He wasn't sure if he'd moved her hand, or if she had. Her eyes softened as her fingers gently stroked his beard stubble.

"I'm sorry. For everything, Rafe."

Chapter Sixteen

Jordan shut her eyes against the onslaught of emotions reeling through her. Anger spiked and throbbed, veering swiftly to shock at her own highly physical response. Rafe's pinked cheek and unfazed response moved her quickly to regret. He did everything but turn and offer his other cheek.

This wasn't like her. This level of anger was foreign. An anger so big she didn't quite know where to put it. She didn't know where to direct it to land safely. But she would not be an out-of-control person who let hostility rule her actions. She was simply sick and exhausted of jerking from desire to anger and reeling right back to desire again. Maybe Rafe was right. This outburst had to happen so they could move past this and move on to…whatever.

They could be friends again, *real* friends, keep in touch and talk occasionally. Now he and Susan would need support, and she could be there for them. In some small way. *After* this wedding. Until then she had no time for anything or anyone else. And yet. She had been gifted with a few hours of uninterrupted time courtesy of an act of God.

She was still touching Rafe, luxuriating in the slight scrape of beard stubble against her fingers. With a boldness she didn't know she had, she tugged on his bottom lip, and sent him an invitation. In one swift move he crushed her against him, hands settling low on her back. The air between them was thick with the same electrical waves that had always sparked between them. She heard hard, uneven breaths, shocked to realize they were coming from her.

He kissed her, hot and fierce, and she wound her arms around his neck, gripping him tightly. His body shook and trembled under her touch, just like hers, and the knowledge filled her with gratification. No matter what else they'd lost, they still had this. This connection that never failed to stun.

His hard and masculine mouth took the kiss deeper. Longer. Her hands slipped under his shirt, touching warm, taut skin and hard muscles that bunched under her touch.

He groaned and pulled his shirt off in one quick move, giving her what she wanted.

"Oh my. Rafe." She covered her smile.

"What?" He cocked his head with a wicked grin.

"You…you're so…*ripped*. I guess I forgot."

He chuckled, then lifted and carried her to bed. "Let me show you what else you might have forgotten."

Outside, a strong wind whipped against the windowpanes, and Jordan and Rafe lay wrapped in each other's arms. Naked as the day they were born. Making up for lost years, they'd gone at lovemaking like two sex-starved prisoners on a conjugal visit. After three times, Jordan finally cried uncle. Rafe might be insatiable, but he'd physically worn her out. She hadn't had this much sex since…well, since the last time she'd been with Rafe.

"What happens now?" Jordan asked lazily.

"You tell me." Rafe played with the soft wisps of hair at her temple. "We figure things out. Together."

"I don't know." Head on his chest, she listened to the thudding of his strong heartbeat. "I was kind of hoping for a fling."

He actually laughed. "You can't be serious."

"It was a thought. Because us? It's going to be hard."

"I didn't say it would be easy."

"Susan isn't going to like this. You and me."

"Why do you say that?"

"Just something I read. Kids want their parents together, no matter what. It's not me personally.

It would be anyone who tries to take her mother's place."

"Baby, I gave the first four years of her life trying to make the marriage work for Susan's sake. And that's all I can give. I threw enough time away. Besides, kids don't get to decide whether they can have candy for dinner. And they don't get to decide if their parents should stay married, either. Not when it's clearly unhealthy for everyone."

"I know, but still… I don't want her to hate me."

"She won't hate you, or don't you realize how much she already likes you?"

"Before I *kissed* her father." She smiled, knowing she'd done a lot more than kiss him. "She thinks we're friends."

"I'll talk to her."

"Don't." Jordan didn't want to change anything too soon because what if this didn't work out? Again? Susan had been through enough changes in her short life. "Not yet."

"When I said I'd talk to her, I meant the preschool version. But whatever you say, as long as I know you'll give us a chance."

He drew her face up to meet his lips and gave her a long and claiming kiss.

And that was the thing about her and Rafe. Without words, they both understood on a deep down and basic level that everything between them had changed. This, whatever *this* was, would not be casual. Not temporary. They had started something new in the past few hours while the wind battered outside, the fires burned and EMS personnel worked to clear the highway.

But she would never have any regrets. They might not work this time around, either, but she'd survived Rafe before, and she'd do it again if she had to. She'd proved her own worth to herself and to others. She would never be the quiet calm girl who went along with a man and his ambitions. He would need to go along with hers, or at least compromise. There was nothing more to prove. She would only answer to herself from this point forward.

And maybe even try to relax a little now and then. She had possibly spent too much time working the past few years. And letting go like she had tonight? Pretty amazing. Highly recommended. She gave it five dazzling stars.

They'd been lying quietly, her head splayed on his chest, his fingers lazily rubbing her back, when her thoughts went back to the wedding.

"Have you written your best man toast yet?"

"Wait. I was supposed to do that?"

She went up on one elbow. "Are you *kidding* me?"

"I'm going to wing it." He smiled lazily.

"Wing it. You're going to *wing* it."

"Those are always the best speeches. I've been thinking about Max, and who he was since the time I met him. How Ava seems to have changed him." He kissed her temple. "For the better, of course. As you women all seem to do."

"So you have a direction. Good."

"I thought about making a bunch of random and crude jokes but then I pictured you. Your beautiful face, puckered lips and narrowed eyes. If you hadn't already slapped me, you would have then."

"Is that how you still see me?" She thought maybe after tonight, possibly she'd shown, instead of told him, that she wasn't too tightly wound. "Difficult and judgmental?"

"I never saw you that way. And I'm kidding about the racy jokes."

"Whew! What a relief." She mopped her brow with exaggeration then lay back down in the crook of his shoulder. "Can I actually get some sleep now?"

"Sure, I'll allow it." He winked and it affected her as much as it might have the waitress ready to have his children.

A squeezing low in her belly. Her heart pounding powerfully. Yes, she might be ready to have his babies.

Whoa, there, Jordan. Slow down before you give yourself whiplash.

Navigating life with a single father and his somewhat bitter ex-wife just might be the biggest challenge of her life. At least she wouldn't have to deal with Liz anytime soon. It seemed naive to hope for never.

She rolled over on her side and Rafe pulled her back to his front. Wrapped in his strong, warm arms, she would have no trouble finding sleep tonight.

"That was a beautiful fairy tale you told Susan. It sounded so…familiar."

"You caught that." His warm breath fanned across her neck and a deep longing hit her hard.

"Do you always make up fairy tales for her on the spot?"

"No. I've been telling her that one for a few years now."

She squeezed her eyes shut, blinking back tears. "Oh, Rafe."

"It's okay." He kissed her bare shoulder, sending soft tendrils of heat.

"I'm the princess."

"How do you know *I'm* not the princess?"

She turned to face him and confirm the smile she'd heard in his voice. "The princess and her big family. Her brother, who was the pauper's best friend. Except you had us married in the story."

"It's feel-good fiction. I started the story with what the toad had but lost. And then gave him a happily-ever-after. And yes, *I'm* the toad."

"Hardly." She framed his face. "You're the best man I know."

"Jordan," he spoke softly, meeting her gaze. "You know I love you. I never stopped."

She kissed him sweetly, and then again, not as sweet.

And she forgot all about sleep.

Rafe startled awake, and when he did, Jordan moaned and rolled out of his arms.

Reluctantly, he rubbed his eyes and glanced at the digital clock. Jordan would want to be on the road soon. No time to wake her up the fun way. He took a shower and dressed quickly, then headed down to see what kind of continental breakfast he could grab for them.

She'd want coffee and so did he. With a little spring in his step, he found a line at the coffee machine. Not too surprising given the full vacancy. He waited in line several minutes for his turn, checking his app and finding the highway open. Hallelujah. Jordan would be pleased.

He wished he could personally thank the EMS personnel who'd shut it down for safety reasons. He and Jordan had needed this time together away from the distractions of a wedding, and a four-year-old, so they could talk. Let down those walls and yell at each other. Thankfully, they'd done a lot more than talk. He'd reached for a personal best in trying to catch up on four years of missing his woman, and how they'd always fit together.

"What are you so happy about?" A senior citizen in front of him turned, holding his Styrofoam cup of coffee, and wearing a sour expression. "Surely you didn't *enjoy* your surprise stay at the Penny Lodge."

Rafe shrugged. "Actually, I did. Guess it's a matter of perspective."

He hummed silently as he carried the coffees back to their room.

Okay, so he had some work ahead of him. His ex-wife wouldn't be thrilled at this reunion with Jordan, whom she irrationally blamed, at least partially, for the dissolution of their marriage. It wasn't fair, but unhappy people were rarely logical in their accusations. Liz would simply get used to the situation, as he had with the man she'd been dating, who kept trying to win Susan's love by buying everything she pointed to in the toy store.

His phone buzzed in his pocket and he set the coffee cups down near the check-in counter. He hadn't even glanced at his cell yet this morning and guilt pulsed through him. What if Cole had been trying to contact him about Susan? Damn it. *Liz* calling. If he didn't answer, she'd accuse him of not keeping communications open between them. He might have a few minutes, but he didn't have much more.

"What's up?" he answered.

"Just called to wish my munchkin a good morning."

"Here's the thing. She's in Charming with Cole and his wife, Valerie. I'm on my way to San Antonio but I should be back in a few hours."

He didn't tell her Susan had spent the night without Rafe. That information was on a need-to-know basis.

"And why are you in San Antonio and our daughter is in Charming without you?"

"As you know, she's not exactly fond of three-hour car rides. *Each* way."

"What's in San Antonio?"

He ignored that. "If you call the lighthouse, the

landline I gave you, you can talk to her and wish her a good morning. She's having a great time. I'm sure she's already asked you about getting a dog."

"Yes, she has, and thank you very much for that."

Rafe winced. "You can always say no. I did."

"Yes, it's so easy for you to say no. But I'm dealing with a little girl upset that her parents are no longer together."

"It's not *easy* for me to say no. Sometimes it's necessary." He wound up lecturing Liz far too often.

"I'm hanging up now," Liz said with irritation.

She'd allowed the guilt of those last two deployments to eat at her, regretful of all the time she'd spent away from Susan in those early years. Possibly jealous or envious of the bond he had with Susan. He slid the cell back into his pocket, picked up the coffees and went on his way. The shower was going when he walked inside, and a few minutes later, Jordan stepped outside the bathroom wrapped in a white towel with green stitching.

She wore an expression too familiar to one he'd seen in the mirror nearly every day of his four-year marriage. It was a "what the hell did I get myself into?" look.

He'd gone back to Watsonville to tell Jordan he would be marrying Liz and watched with shock as Jordan begged him not to. The knowledge had sunk him. Because Jordan still loved him, and it was too late. He'd made a promise.

If her memories of that horrible day were as

strong as his, Jordan was probably now terrified she'd stepped right back into the same place of pain and loss.

Worried this one night had been an awful mistake.

"Hey," he said, pulling her into his arms.

He held her against his chest, lowering his chin to her shoulders. She'd told him once, he gave the best hugs, and right now, he had something to prove. Her shoulders and neck were damp, her cheeks flushed and pink. She smelled like soap and her own special Jordan scent that had somehow always reminded him of strawberries.

"Rafe," she whispered into his chest. "What the devil did we do?"

"I don't know about you, but for me? Last night was everything I dreamed and fantasized about for years." His mouth moved to her neck and slid across her sweet, damp skin.

"*Everyone* is going to hate us. My parents, Max, Susan. Liz. I'm not supposed to be with you. I'm not supposed to love you. We finally all got to a place of healing and forgiveness."

"I don't care about any of that. Jordan." He tugged on the nape of her neck, forcing her to meet his gaze. "Do you love me?"

He might not have asked the question if he didn't already see the answer in her eyes. If he could not already sense it by the way she'd responded to him, with every move of her sensual and perfect body.

It seemed to take forever before she spoke, but it might have only been a second.

"Yes. Of course, I do. I'm in love with you."

"Stay with me. Don't be afraid. I'm with you, and we're going to make this work. Or I swear to you, I'll die trying."

A smile tugged at her lips. "Promise?"

"Yes. Now, you do something for me."

"Sure."

He smiled. "Drop the towel."

Chapter Seventeen

Not only did they get a late start, but Jordan and Rafe nearly missed checkout time, too busy twisting up the sheets. By the time they walked outside, the parking lot was nearly empty, everyone already cleared out. According to Rafe, the highway had been open for hours. It had opened sometime during the wee morning hours when they'd been sleeping, or... you know, *not* sleeping.

"Next time I'm taking you someplace a lot nicer than this," Rafe said as he held the door open for her.

She squeezed his arm. "Not like you planned for any of this."

And for a person who had created an entire career out of her love of organizing, the whole unforeseeable event had been nothing less than humbling. No one could plan for every eventuality. She would have to learn how to better switch gears and understand not everything in the world had an alternate plan. Her life had recently gone off the rails, for instance, through no planning. She'd had a zero-alternative plan for Rafe.

First, he was supposed to be married. Second, he was supposed to stay away from her, busy with his daughter. Lastly, she wasn't supposed to still love him.

If Maribel or anyone else had suggested Jordan would arrive in Charming and reunite with Rafe, she would have asked them what they were smoking in that pipe. Of all the people in her family, only Maribel might be happy about this. But even she would be genuinely surprised.

Jordan's head was spinning with this tenuous reconciliation. Rafe said he'd never stopped loving her and the story he'd told Susan over the phone hurt her heart. It was so clearly their story. Their broken fairy tale. And though she wanted badly to believe in happily-ever-after, she was a little jaded now. Nothing would ever be simple or easy with them. They'd both walked through a minefield, endured the explosion and would now try to put the old and fractured back together again.

It simply wouldn't look the same.

It wasn't only Rafe that had changed by marrying, divorcing and becoming a single father. By choosing to leave the military and settle down in one place. She'd changed, too, from the easygoing girl who planned parties and enjoyed them to an obsessed event planner who rarely had much fun. She supposed Maribel was right and Jordan had needed to cut loose.

The florist in San Antonio was easy enough to locate off the main highway, and the owner apologetic over not being able to personally make the delivery.

"No apology necessary. You really helped me out of a jam," Jordan said. "Thank you for taking the order."

"It's all ready for you. I'm sorry, but we were out of sunflowers and they're so difficult to work with. I think these yellow daisies really fit the bill."

Jordan had to admit they looked nicer than she would have expected. Daisies were normally such ordinary flowers, but in the right setting, they could certainly shine. Most importantly, Ava's bouquet was still the arrangement ordered. Beautiful baby's breath with miniature red roses.

Rafe helped the clerk load the van with the flowers, which took up the entirety of the lowered back seats. A few minutes later, they started the long drive back to Charming. This time an easy silence fell between them, punctuated by Rafe occasionally picking up her hand to brush a kiss across her knuckles.

Without traffic, they'd arrive this afternoon well before dinner. While Rafe drove, Jordan made her calls. She reassured Ava that the flowers were beautiful, and they would arrive in plenty of time.

"And I'll talk to your father tonight. I already

found another DJ. It's the same one Rafe hired for the rehearsal."

"What would I do without you?" Ava gushed.

"Well, you won't have to find out."

After Jordan hung up, Rafe spoke up. "Let *me* talk to Dr. Long."

Visions of Max barreling in and ordering Dr. Long to cancel the jazz quartet flashed in her mind. There was a reason Rafe and Max had been best friends forever. She searched for a reason to tell Rafe this was a bad idea without hurting his feelings.

"I can talk to him, from one father of a daughter to another. It's her day, right, so everything should be as she wants."

Interesting. From one father to another. Why didn't she think of that?

"Can you do it with finesse, so he thinks it was his idea in the first place?"

"Well, I'm no Jordan Del Toro, but I'll do it. In my own style."

"*Your* style? What does that mean?"

"Well, baby, I have a four-year-old. I will make suggestions, I will encourage, support and listen. And if I have to, I *will* beg."

The drive back to Charming was notably different than the drive up. Rafe stopped for gas, bought snacks and they talked for all three hours, the music off. Avoiding the minefields, they caught up on each other's lives. Jordan confirmed that Rafe had retired early from service purely so Liz could do two more deployments. He took care of Susan himself in the first year, with only occasional help from his mother when she'd fly out to see them. Jordan's respect for him grew exponentially with each tiny detail she learned.

She caught him up on her life, post-breakup, somehow far too easy when compared to Rafe's. She told him how and when she'd decided to start her own business, catching the spirit of an entrepreneur by beginning to truly understand herself. One thing they did not discuss: plans for their future.

"Head to the bar," Jordan said when they neared Charming. "I've already talked to Adam about storing the flowers in their spare refrigerator. The hotel has also offered us some room."

As they rode down the winding strip of road that faced the beach, Jordan noticed a few cottages. They were probably rentals for tourists. Maybe next time she visited Max and Ava, Jordan would rent a cottage. She pictured two Adirondack chairs side by side, burying her feet in the sand, listening to the soothing waves. Heaven.

Wonder if Rafe and Susan would come with her. Autumn would be better than summer, for heat, and other considerations. Maybe even winter. She'd have to look into rates and find out if these cottages were temporary or long-term rentals. Perhaps someday she'd look into buying a vacation home here, once her business was more sustainable, and she'd hired a bigger staff.

Damn, there you go planning your future again.

It was like a sickness. She had to let go. Relax. Let life unfold.

"I am beginning to love this town," Rafe said, echoing her thoughts.

She snorted, because really, who wouldn't? Even with heat and humidity this place grew on a person. Delved deep into one's soul and made a nest there.

"Why? Is it the atmosphere? The people? The bucolic ambience and coastal views? The lighthouse? The beautiful seawall? The boardwalk with carnival-style rides and cotton candy?"

He quirked a brow and slid her an easy smile. "All of the above, but what I'll never forget is this was the place where I saw you again."

"In the bridal shop." She lowered her gaze. "I'm sorry I avoided you. I thought you were married. Then I thought you were flirting with the salesclerk, and when I saw you at the Salty Dog with her, I assumed..."

He reached for her hand, squeezed it. "Jordan, the past few years have been all about trying to get over you. I thought you were almost engaged, remember?"

They arrived at the bar and grill at what appeared to be a lull between their lunch and dinner hours. Only a few people were seated at booths, lingering over their food. Chatting quietly.

"Hey, guys." Adam met them at the entrance, fist-bumped with Rafe and helped him get the flowers loaded.

"Make sure you place the bouquets separately."

Jordan directed them until she realized she sounded a tad compulsive. Adam gave her a furrowed brow that telegraphed he had this handled, thank you very much. She got the message.

"Okay, okay." She went hands up. "I'll just get out of your way and wait over here."

No sooner was she seated than Debbie appeared with her trusty apron and Salty Dog T-shirt of a bulldog. "Hey, hon. What are ya havin'?"

"Nothing for me. I have to get going right after the guys refrigerate the flowers in the back."

Debbie cocked her head. "Hey, you look nice today. Is that a new hairdo or somethin'?"

Jordan smoothed down the wild hair she'd tamed into a ponytail this morning when she came out of the shower without any of her products. Debbie had to be joking.

"Um, no."

"Well, something is different. You look, I don't know…forgive me, honey, but you always look so *tense*. Maybe that's it. You're more relaxed now, I think."

Of course she was more at ease. Smooth sailing from here on out.

"Wedding day is almost here. I mean, what else can go wrong?" Jordan laughed.

Debbie blinked. "Don't ask. Thirty-two years ago, when I got married, my husband dropped the ring. That sounds like a small thing, sure, but we couldn't find it for thirty minutes. Oh, and also, we married during a hurricane."

Jordan swallowed over the pebble in her throat. "W-what?"

"Yep, should have known then it was going to be a humdinger of a marriage. Never a bored day in my life, I'll say that. We went ahead with the wedding, in the basement of the church. Oh, we were all safe, don't give me that look. I was six weeks pregnant, and we figured we better get on with it. The pastor and my mama were already suspicious."

"I'm sorry. That's…less than ideal."

"We didn't have a wedding planner, or she might have told us *not* to get married during hurricane season. But then again…" She patted her tummy, then waved and went to her next customers.

Jordan scrolled through her phone while she waited. The bachelor and bachelorette parties were tonight, to give everyone an extra day—at Jordan's recommendation—just in case someone was too hung over. That wouldn't happen in this case, but best to prepare for every eventuality. If Cole, Adam, Rafe or Max threw up on the altar, all parents, not to mention the bride, would be mortified.

The caterers had confirmed and would be setting up in the hotel's banquet hall tomorrow, and the ice sculpture would be arriving on the morning of the wedding. Jordan ticked it all off in her mind to avoid responding to Maribel's text, sent late last night when Jordan was otherwise…occupied. Ahem.

Excuse me? You're spending the night with Rafe? What?!

By now Maribel had all the details from Cole, and Jordan carefully composed her reply:

Yes.

Maribel shot back: That's all you got for me? Yes?
The text was followed by an exploding head emoji and about a bazillion question marks.
Jordan responded:

What makes you think I slept with him? What if we were in two separate hotel rooms? Did you ever think of that?!

She followed with the wearing dark shades "cool" emoji and the shrugging emoji.

Were you? In separate rooms?

Jordan swallowed thickly at her sister's questions and replied:

No.

The resulting incoming call from Maribel was not all that surprising.
"Hello," Jordan answered, observing Rafe and

Adam chatting in the back. "I can't talk. Rafe will be here in a minute."

"Okay. Just answer one question—are you happy about this? Or are you overthinking?"

Jordan was both happy and also overthinking because, hello, overachiever. "Um, both?"

"That's what I thought. *Chica*, don't *think* too much. Just have fun with Rafe. He's hot, a good guy and you need a fling."

Jordan winced. "I don't think this can be a *fling*."

"Why am I not surprised? You don't do temporary, that's why."

"And neither does Rafe. He's a single dad, or did you forget?"

"How could I *forget*? Susan drove us all batty last night. Why, why, why. If only I could bottle her energy."

"And was she okay this morning?"

"I don't know. I left right after she finally fell asleep. Apparently Rafe told her a story over the phone and then she went to sleep. She said her daddy always tells the best stories. When I told her it might be rude to say that in front of Valerie, because she was trying, Susan said she could *never* tell a lie." Maribel chuckled.

"Zero filter."

"None at all. You *remember* that when she says something completely unfiltered about you."

Jordan sighed. "I'll try."

Rafe walked toward Jordan.

"Talk later."

"Yes, we will. Maybe at the party tonight, where I'll pump you full of cocktails."

"Don't you dare. This is Ava's night." With that, she disconnected and stood.

"Ready?"

Rafe held out his hand, and even though she knew everyone, including Adam, was probably watching them, she took it.

Chapter Eighteen

"Daddy, are you going to be back in time to tell me a story and tuck me in?" Later in the afternoon, Susan skipped along the beach in front of him, waving her magic wand.

Rafe had already reassured her repeatedly that he was not going to leave her again overnight. However, even if this night had actually been planned, it would still make two nights in a row he'd be out. This probably wouldn't win him any father of the year awards, but he was determined to have a social life again. He'd given up so much of his life for Susan and had been happy to do it. But now it was time to reclaim a part of his life he should have never let go of in the first place.

Earlier, he'd dropped off Jordan at her hotel room,

and they'd both been very good at keeping their hands to themselves. Other than a passionate "see you later" kiss in the hallway, he practically deserved to be awarded angel's wings for his self-control. Now he had only a matter of days to figure out how to keep her.

He wasn't stupid enough to ask her to abandon her career and plans in California. Because of Liz, he was stuck in Dallas for the foreseeable future. Unless he could talk her into moving to California to be near his mother for a change. And Jordan.

"Hey, Shortie, do you like my friend Jordan?" He bent to reach for a piece of driftwood and threw it ahead for Sub.

"Yeah, I like her. She's my new friend. I told Mommy."

He cleared his throat, not having any doubt how well that had gone over with Liz.

"I would like to spend more time with her. Maybe all three of us together."

Susan gave him a funny look, her eyebrows quirked. It was as if she'd read his mind.

He had no idea *what* he was doing. He should google "how to introduce your daughter to the love of your life, the woman who *isn't* her mother." Surely there was a boatload of information on the subject. He wasn't the first man who'd totally screwed up with love.

"What about Mommy?" Susan asked.

"What about her?"

"Can she come, too?"

"Mommy probably wants to spend time with you and Carl. You know, her boyfriend." He hoped Susan would read between the lines. She was as bright as they came.

"But Carl is ugly." Susan pouted. "I hate him."

This wasn't true. In fact, Susan liked Carl most of the time. "It's not nice to call someone ugly."

"I could *never* tell a lie."

Rafe snorted and internally rolled his eyes. "Good, but that's not the same thing. You can be honest and still be kind."

Sub barked at the waves and chased a few seagulls. For the next few hours, Rafe built sandcastles, looked for seashells and mermaids, and waded into the warm gulf waters with Susan on his shoulders. She wore her water wings because she wasn't a strong enough swimmer for his liking, and Rafe stayed close as she swam in shallow water.

This beach reminded him a little of another one, near Watsonville, where he'd grown up. A small farm town along the coast, it would be the perfect place to raise a child. But if Liz knew Rafe wanted to move back to California because of Jordan, she'd never agree to it. Instead, he'd need to continue to sell her on the area. The advantages of being near his side of the family, and the only grandmother Susan had. The only other grandparent Susan had left was Kelly's father, who had never made much time for her.

None of this would be easy. He could already feel

the weight of resistance all the way from Dallas. Liz would suggest *he* move to Watsonville if that was what he wanted.

But if he moved to California, he would be lucky to get summers with Susan. He didn't know if he'd be content with being a summertime father anyway. He was already a weekend father, this week being the most time he'd spent with Susan since the separation. On the other hand, he couldn't be fulfilled if he continued to sacrifice his own happiness for Susan. And if his friends with older children were right, the day when she'd likely appreciate what he'd done was decades away. He still had the teenage years to get through.

It wasn't that he needed anyone to thank him for what he'd sacrificed, least of all Susan. It was, simply put, that he finally wanted his own life. And he'd prefer to have his old life back, pre-Susan. Maybe, just maybe, that wasn't too much to ask.

He recalled his own mother saying to him on her last visit to Dallas, "You deserve to be happy. Sacrificing for your children can only go so far. Take it from me. They will sense your unhappiness at not having a full life of your own."

Everything he'd read post-divorce about coparenting said that a happy parent was also a happy and well-adjusted child. But putting this into practice was a bit like juggling knives. While they were on fire.

When he and Susan returned to the lighthouse,

Valerie had finished the setup for tonight's bach-elorette party. The lower room had been converted into a spa of sorts where he'd been told the women would get facials, back massages and mani-pedis.

"Are you ready for your manicure?" Valerie bent and tweaked Susan's nose.

"Yes! And I want pink with glitter. Lots and lots of glitter." She twirled around in a circle.

"Oh, boy." Rafe tousled her hair.

He was fortunate to have these friends in his life and their low-key, child-friendly party. Through Cole, Max's mother had actually offered to baby-sit Susan, gratifying Rafe with the knowledge they wouldn't hold anything against Susan no matter how they felt about him. Even if they had yet to say a sin-gle word to him. The senior citizens of the Almost Dead Poet Society, who were watching Tennessee, had also offered. But once his girly-girl found out about the nail polish, she'd begged to stay. Valerie, the saint, said it would be fine.

Cole hurried down the staircase, dressed in his usual casual beach bum vibe but brandishing cigars. "Are we ready for tonight?"

"Please don't drink too much," Valerie said, com-ing to her tiptoes to plant a kiss on his lips. "You're sleeping on the couch if you even have the slight stink of whiskey on you."

"I'll drink tequila." Cole grinned.

After a quick shower and change, Rafe and Cole

both said their goodbyes and went off to meet the entire groom's party at the Salty Dog.

Jordan relaxed under the warm towel covering her face. Every muscle in her body untensed and unclenched. She should do this kind of thing more often. Make time for it in her busy schedule. She hadn't been pampered this way in years.

Facials, mani-pedis, a sundae ice cream bar, wine coolers, followed by a steady stream of rom-coms playing on the flat screen as background. She was in heaven and couldn't have done a better job of planning the bachelorette party than Valerie. She had a teacher friend who'd decided to open up her own day spa, and so she had the local connections.

Even both Dr. Longs, Ava's parents, were suitably impressed, and Jordan imagined they spent a great deal of their free time getting pampered. The only complaint Jordan had heard, said in hushed tones, was that a child should not be allowed to run around willy-nilly. She'd felt defensive on Rafe's behalf. Susan was behaving herself and quite entertaining.

"I'm so glad Valerie is the maid of honor," Maribel said lazily from the table next to her, where she was getting a massage. "No offense."

"None taken. And I just got a few new ideas for spa day parties." Early in her business, Jordan had done more themed parties before she'd begun to specialize in weddings.

"I can't believe you're still thinking about work."

"That's not fair. This is the nature of my business. But I am relaxing. I swear."

"Do a lot more relaxing and less thinking about business."

"Maribel, I'm *not* a workaholic. I just maybe… hadn't quite achieved a perfect work-life balance. Did it ever occur to you it's because I like what I do?"

"And now you are a *fairy princess*!" Susan spoke loudly and tapped her wand on Maribel's head for the countless time.

"Thank you, ma'am," said Maribel.

Previously, she'd been a toad, a Power Ranger, Elsa, Snow White, a dwarf and a woodland creature. Meanwhile, Jordan had been turned into a rainbow unicorn. Not surprisingly, the girl was hopped up on sugar, glitter and nail polish. Valerie was allowing her to stay up until Rafe came home to put her to bed. If she lasted that long.

Jordan wondered if she should try and put Susan to bed. If Jordan was ever going to be a part of her daily life, it might be good to know how to do these… things. Still, as Maribel had warned her earlier tonight, she shouldn't get ahead of herself.

"This isn't going to be easy," Maribel had counseled earlier this evening. "I mean, I'll be happy if it works out for you, but…"

"But…?"

"Rafe has an ex-wife. There's lots to navigate in blended families. Are you ready for all that?"

No. She wasn't, but how could one ever be ready?

Was there a course you took somewhere before you fell in love with a single dad? Probably *not*.

"Remember I once dated a guy with children. It's very attractive in the beginning, until you spend all your weekends at soccer games. Broken dates because the kid is throwing up. Rearranged trips because the ex-wife wanted to switch weekends. Even if he's a weekend dad, the children always have to come first."

"I would never ask Rafe to put me before his own daughter."

"No, of course not. But I'm just saying…it's not a great feeling when you always take a back seat. Plus, this is *Liz's* daughter."

"*And* Travis."

"Well, unfortunately, he's not around anymore."

Just then, someone shouted from outside, interrupting Jordan's thoughts.

"Ava!"

Jordan removed the towel from her face and sat up ramrod straight. That was Max's voice. She'd know it anywhere.

"Max?" said Maribel, also recognizing the voice. "What the devil—"

Great. What in the world was wrong? An emergency? She would fix this. Jordan scrambled off the table and went to the window with everyone else.

"Look, it's Daddy!" Susan pointed. "He came back to tell me my story."

And indeed, Max stood between Rafe and Adam.

Cole was sitting on one of the Adirondack chairs smoking a cigar, and the rest of the men were admiring the lighthouse and pointing at different angles.

"Ava, I love you! Marry me!" Max shouted.

"Oh my god, my brother is *such* a dweeb." Maribel covered her face with both hands. "How humiliating."

"Is he…singing?" Jordan clutched her chest.

"Oh, look how handsome he is!" Ava gushed. "I haven't seen him for two days and I swear he got… handsomer?"

"Two *days*?" Maribel asked. "Why haven't you seen him for two days?"

"Well, we're trying this thing where we're apart until the wedding day." Ava's cheeks pinked. "It's been…tough."

Jordan met Maribel's eyes. "Well, *this* explains a lot."

"I say we ignore them," said Ava's sister-in-law from under the masseuse's talented hands. "I never get enough 'me time' anymore."

But it didn't matter what any of them thought because Ava had already rushed outside. She was currently being lifted several feet above the ground in Max's arms.

"Oh, well. That *is* kind of sweet," Maribel murmured.

Jordan didn't bother to agree because she'd met Rafe's eyes through the big picture window. He didn't break eye contact, giving her a shoulder shrug and a slow smile. Then he subtly beckoned her outside.

"Let me just see what this is all about." Jordan cleared her throat.

"Yeah, you do that." Maribel smirked and hooked her thumb to the masseuse. "I'll just be in here with my new best friend."

Outside, the night was cool and clear. Stars sparkled in the black velvet sky. And the man who'd captured her attention stood as if he waited for her. Valerie was already sitting on Cole's lap as he grinned like the cat who'd captured the canary. Stacy and Adam were walking hand in hand along the beach, oblivious to anyone else. The rest of the men were slowly making their way inside the house.

Susan danced in a circle around Rafe, waving her wand. "And *you* are a prince!"

Oh, yes he is.

How had she ever imagined she could replace this man with someone, with *anyone* else? He'd been her heart for the entirety of her youth. They were both older now, wiser and certainly…damaged. But there remained something real, on a soul-deep level, that could be put back together.

Because yes, she loved him. She adored him. No doubt remained that her heart would always have a place for Rafe. Her heart would always beat for him. Her soul would always recognize his. She'd managed to keep him out of her mind for years by focusing obsessively on the minutiae of life. By pushing to be the best version of herself, even if all the work she'd done was on the outside. Success measured *solely* by achievements. But in all that time, she hadn't actually healed her heart. She'd slapped a Band-Aid on it and called it a day.

Rafe held out his hand for her. "Believe me, I tried to stop him, but he wanted to see Ava. And you know how your brother is when he sets his mind to something."

Jordan took his hand, sending him a smile. "This is not the purpose and intent behind bachelor and bachelorette parties."

"What, you've never attended one where the groom would rather spend time with his bride than a bunch of salty men? That's *shocking*."

"Tell me the truth. How much has he been drinking?" Jordan turned to watch Max and Ava, locked in a clinch.

"Enough so I wouldn't let him drive, but don't worry." Rafe threw a look in Max's direction. "He knows *exactly* what he's doing. And exactly who he wants."

"Yes." Jordan acknowledged, watching the two wrapped in each other's arms. "They have what I've always wanted."

"We had that." He squeezed her hand. "And we lost it."

"Boo!" Susan said, playfully coming between them. "I scared you. It's dark and I scared you because you couldn't see me."

"That's right. I didn't see or hear you," Rafe said but his gaze never left Jordan's. "Shortie, you really should get to sleep now."

"Could I have eleventy more minutes?"

"Eleven," Rafe said firmly.

Jordan eyed him for a long beat when Susan danced away. "That's weirdly *precise*."

"That's Susan."

"I have eleventy minutes," Susan happily informed Valerie. "That's a long time."

Jordan chuckled. "It sounds as though she can't actually tell time, so that's a relief. I worry she'll soon outsmart me."

"Nope, her eleven minutes are five of mine." Rafe gave a slow smile. "Depending on how tired I am."

"Are you tired, Rafe?" She cocked her head.

This time the flirty tone was hers, as she allowed herself to picture Rafe *not* wearing his shirt.

He grinned, equal parts flirty and sexy. "Not even close."

Chapter Nineteen

Rafe softly shut the bedroom door. Hopped up on sugar, Susan had eventually worn herself out to the point where she'd fallen asleep before he got to the end of his messed-up fairy tale. Someday, he imagined when she was much older, he'd tell her about the *real* toad in the story. Not so she could thank him for helping raise her or acknowledge some great sacrifice he'd made. He didn't need to be thanked, but he did want Susan to someday understand why he and Liz had never belonged together. Why they could have never worked even with a thousand marriage counselors in their corner.

Liz had lost the love of her life, but he had not. He'd been in love with someone else who was not his wife. For most of his life, from the moment he'd understood the meaning of falling in love, he'd loved

Jordan Del Toro. Yes, they'd been on and off a few times when he'd deployed and had not wanted her to sit around and hope he'd return intact from whatever conflict.

He'd briefly been with other women, no strings on both sides, and none were memorable. She'd also had the freedom to find someone else, and he always secretly worried she would. Instead, when he returned, they always found a way back to each other.

Had he been able to choose whom he could love for a lifetime, he might have chosen Liz, because they made sense. Both retired military personnel, with similar temperaments and views of the world. A little girl in common they would do anything for. But a heart didn't always listen to reason. His own feelings had been far more complicated and chaotic than he'd wanted them to be. Once, he thought he'd had tight control over his life. But he had no control when it came to Jordan and had never managed to get her out of his system. And he was done trying.

Because now he no longer wanted to try.

Unfortunately, he had enough baggage to fill an airport carousel by himself. He might no longer look like the best match for Jordan, but damn if he would give up on them. He'd spend the rest of his life trying to be the best man for her. It would be up to her to decide if she couldn't put up with his lifetime commitment to co-parenting. He couldn't change this, nor did he want to. Liz would always be in his life.

And because she was Susan's mother, he'd never speak ill of her no matter how he occasionally felt.

Downstairs, the cleanup had begun and Rafe jumped in to help. The job went quickly with everyone but Max and Ava helping because no one would allow them to. Instead, they were hanging out somewhere on the beach probably making out in a secluded spot. Adam and Stacy left with plans to stop by the bar and take care of any loose ends there before they went home to their baby girl.

"Do you want to go for a walk?" Rafe asked Jordan when they both finished putting away the last of the dishes.

"It's late," she said, casting her eyes toward Maribel, who had curled up on the couch with her eyes closed. "We drove together. I should take her back."

"Just a short one." He held out his hand, and to his good fortune, she took it.

He appreciated a clear night like the one they'd been gifted tonight. There was so much to be grateful for. This time with Jordan. Celebrating his oldest friend's marriage to the love of his life. A gorgeous beach. Perfect weather. The perfect woman for him. They walked along the edge of the surf, holding hands, until he stopped several yards away from the lighthouse. A ray of moonlight caught a glint of Jordan's dark hair and she smiled up at him.

His hand on the nape of her neck, he hauled her close. Fingers curled through her thick hair, and he kissed her, long and deep, like he'd wanted to do all night. She responded by going all in with him, hands fisted to his shirt. Longing and lust struck him all at once, real and raw. Powerful.

"What's going on here?" Max's voice came out of the quiet evening, irritation clear.

They broke apart then but Rafe kept a hand on Jordan's waist.

"Let me explain," Jordan said.

But Max wasn't looking at Jordan. Instead, his gaze had locked in on Rafe and he felt it to the marrow. *He* was the target. He might be the beneficiary of a devastating explosion unless he found a way to detonate this bomb. Fast.

Ava pulled on Max's arm. "Let's go back to the house."

But Max chose this *particular* moment to ignore his bride for the first time this evening. "Rafe. You, explain."

"Yeah. I will. We—"

"Wait. Is this what I think it is?" Max interrupted, pointing between them, not bothering to wait for an answer. "Here we go again?"

Jordan was biting her lower lip, eyes rounded in concern. Her hands fluttered at her side, as if trying to come up with plausible deniability.

Once, as boys, he and Max had done the stupid childhood small cut on each hand to become "blood" brothers. But no matter how close they'd once been, the separation and distinction between them had always been clear. Even though they'd both excelled and pushed each other to succeed, both enlisting in the service, Max became a SEAL and Rafe a tactical explosives expert. Max came from a large family, and Rafe, just him and his mother. Rafe had met the love of his life as a teenager, and Max not until he met Ava.

They were different, but Rafe knew Max could still read his mind at times. So he let him.

"It's *exactly* what you think." Rafe straightened and his hand curled around Jordan's waist. "If I'm lucky."

Max came at Rafe and grabbed him in a bear hug. "It's about damn time! And don't either one of you screw it up."

Rafe heard the sound both women made as they gasped and laughed in relief.

Gratitude poured through Rafe. Max had never been the alpha, somewhat brain-dead brother to declare "hands off" any of his sisters. He'd always understood it was their decision to make, though he might have felt differently with a player. Then again, Max always picked his friends wisely.

Max hugged Jordan next. "He's the best man I know."

Ava hugged Jordan, then Rafe. "I'm glad this happened during our wedding week. It's the best gift *ever*!"

Rafe tugged Jordan into his arms and pressed a kiss to her temple. He spoke softly in her ear so only she heard him.

"I'm so glad your brother is a happy drunk."

* * *

It's going to be all right.

Jordan let out a deep breath. She released a worry she didn't realize she'd been holding. A thread in her carefully ordered world had threatened to unwind the moment she'd seen Rafe again.

If she gave him another chance, did that make her somehow irresponsible? Foolish? Careless?

Was the risk too much, or just enough of a chance? Only she had the answer to the question. Not Max, her parents or anyone else. Her brother had always been wise enough to stay out of her way and let her make decisions. After all, she had to live with them.

Increasingly, it felt as though Rafe had given her no reason to doubt he wanted a second chance. She wanted to believe. He'd given her the words she needed to hear but now the proof would be in his actions.

Later, on the drive back to the hotel, Maribel grilled Jordan. Her sister had noticed, naturally, that everything between Jordan and Rafe seemed to be moving at roughly the speed of light. Sometimes it felt as if they'd never actually stopped seeing each other. Because after four years of separation, in some ways this was similar to the times he'd been gone for a long deployment.

Then, the air had been charged and thick and heavy between them. On his return from a mission, Rafe was broody, quiet and withdrawn. But eventually he'd open up to Jordan. They'd slowly inched their way back to each other. Discovering each other all over again. It wouldn't be the same this time. Not at all. Rafe had lived a full life without her, and there was a little girl now at the center of his heart.

"Have you talked about how you and Rafe are going to do this?"

"No, we haven't made any…um, plans." It was a bit of an internal shock to her system that *she* didn't have a plan.

She hadn't made a plan.

"Whoa. That doesn't sound like you."

"Right? But damn it, everything I do professionally involves planning. How did I let it take over my life, too?"

"That's been my question all along. Maybe because you had something to prove?"

"Maybe. I went from the girl who just coasted through life from one party to the next with no real goals and ambitions. But a plan doesn't always mean things won't go terribly wrong. I mean, look at me and Geoff. I thought we were made for each other. We planned everything down to the last detail."

"Ahem," Maribel said. "But you forgot to pencil in falling in love. That's something you *can't* plan."

Lesson learned. You couldn't control or choose who you fell in love with, and she and Rafe were one big bowl of spicy complications with a side of freshly tossed anxiety.

"I wish this could be easier."

"I don't know about easy," Maribel said, rolling

down the window of the rental and letting in the salty, cool air. "But when I see Ava and Max, I think…well, it might be worth it."

True enough. Jordan rarely saw any two people more in love. The marriage part was simply a formality. They would be together forever, Jordan was certain.

As for her and Rafe, taking it slow and easy was one thing. Walking into the pitch dark was another. They would need to discuss a few things. Would long-distance work? They'd spent large stretches of time apart when they were younger, but Jordan had never thought of it as ideal.

Did Rafe picture always living in Dallas or could he relocate back to California someday? Was Jordan expected to give up all the business contacts she had and start over in Texas just to be with him?

She had questions, and concerns, but these would be addressed *after* the wedding.

Chapter Twenty

On wedding day, Jordan woke earlier than usual, minus the heart-pounding fear of something going horribly wrong. Undoubtedly, some little thing here or there would be a miss or a near miss, but nothing important. Flowers, check. DJ, check. Caterer, check. Ice sculpture, check. Wedding favors, check. Videographer, check. Her new lists were checked, and triple-checked in the new planner that never failed to draw a smile out of her.

At some point, she shoved a roll down along with her coffee just so she wouldn't be functioning purely on adrenaline and caffeine. She showered and dressed, checking the banquet room one last time before she met her family in the lobby for the limo ride to the church. Maribel stood with the rest of the family, dressed in the same beautifully tailored royal blue gown.

"Leave it to Ava to choose bridesmaid gowns that makes us all look like movie stars." Maribel smoothed down her long skirt and did a little spin. "I love my new sister."

Their mother bustled over. "You both look beautiful. Jordan, I need to talk to you."

"Now?" Jordan swallowed. "We're waiting for the car. It will be here any minute."

"You don't have a minute for your *mami*?" Emilia Del Toro quirked a dark and heavily penciled-in brow. She was *not* someone Jordan could put off for long.

Jordan glanced at the time. "Sure, of course I do."

As the others waited, her mother pulled Jordan aside. "We haven't had any time to talk or spend time together."

"It's been a whirlwind, that's for sure."

"I heard about the flowers." This was said with the same tone one might say, "I heard you were fired from your job for stealing."

"It was a near disaster, but we fixed it."

"You and *Rafe*."

Here came the pursed lips. The *disapproval*. Rafe had broken her daughter's heart and since that moment, Emilia Del Toro's estimation of him was no higher than the disgusting gum she occasionally had the misfortune of accidentally stepping on.

But Jordan knew something her mother would not

easily admit. She'd been terribly invested in Jordan and Rafe, the young man she considered another son. When he married someone else, she'd taken the news nearly as hard as Jordan. The pain had been personal.

It hadn't mattered that Jordan had broken it off with Rafe first.

"Um, yes. I was going to talk to you about him."

"*Why* would you be friendly with Rafe?"

"Well, I needed his help, and he was there for me. He is the best man, after all."

"For your brother. You know Max. It's one of those macho things I don't understand. The brotherhood. But us Del Toro women, we're smarter than that."

"Smarter than…" Jordan let the rest of the sentence die.

"Giving someone who *hurt* us yet another chance."

"Well…" Jordan swallowed thickly. "Don't forget we hurt each other."

Her mother crossed her arms. "Whatever happened to Geoff, that lovely man?"

"He couldn't make it to the wedding."

"Ah, yes." She nodded. "He's so busy."

"That's not really an excuse. He's known about this wedding for a year. He didn't manage to make me, or Max's wedding, a priority. And he *knew* how important this was for me. For us all. This is our family."

Her mother blinked as if this did not compute. Probably because after the Max fiasco, Jordan had stopped sharing details of her love life. Her mother saw Geoff at family functions where they had chatted without ever going too deep. The only family member Jordan confided in on a regular basis was her sister. Maribel knew where all the old planners were buried.

"It's interesting how you make excuses for Geoff but none for Rafe."

"Geoff didn't marry someone *else*."

"And he didn't marry me, either. When we talked about setting a wedding date, he checked his schedule, and thought maybe he could fit us in in two years. Two years! That's how much he wanted to marry me. I had to fit into *his* schedule."

"Madre de Dios!" Emilia clutched her chest.

"It wasn't the two years. That's not the real reason I broke it off with him. I wasn't important. Never was. And… I don't love him enough to wait. *That's* the real problem."

"I understand. But—"

"Here's the thing. It's been hard for me to understand, too, but I see clearer now what Rafe tried to do. He didn't have a father growing up, and he didn't want that for Susan. It was extreme, yes, and you and I don't understand it. It's just another one of those brotherhood things."

Jordan took a breath because suddenly, she was on a roll. The acceptance and knowledge were flowing, and the freedom purely intoxicating.

"And I know what it's like to love someone with all my heart. It isn't Geoff."

"No?"

"I *wish* I loved him and he had truly loved me. My life would sure be easier in some ways."

She tilted her head. "Easier than loving Rafe."

"I've loved him all my life. Maybe I don't know how to stop."

"I'm so sorry, *mija*." Her mother reached to tuck a hair behind Jordan's ear. "Rafe has a daughter and an ex-wife. I had hoped love would be simpler for you."

"You know what? Me, too." Jordan chuckled. "Me too."

Only while in the limo on the way to the church had Jordan remembered the *string quartet*. She'd nearly had to find a paper bag to breathe into, but after a frantic text to Rafe, he confirmed that yes, he'd already talked to Dr. Long. The quartet would be performing as guests were seated in the church. A perfect compromise.

And so, the Long–Del Toro wedding ceremony went forth smoothly.

Ava beamed as she strolled down the aisle and Jordan thought she might have actually caught tears in her big brother's eyes when his bride joined him at the altar. Dr. Long, the mother, dispensed tissues to both Lucia and Jordan's mother, then dabbed at her own eyes.

Jordan tightly held her bouquet, trying her best to give all her attention to the exchange of vows. This was a sacred time. But it was difficult not to stare at

Rafe, to study his strong jawline and firm mouth. He lowered his head as the vows were exchanged and she wished she could read his thoughts.

Are you thinking what I am? This might have been us?

The wedding was beautiful.

Next, the reception, which could be a very different story. In Jordan's experience, this was often where all the trouble began. And alcohol played a key role.

The first issue became the intricate ice sculpture of two doves taking flight, a ribbon between them.

"Is that...*melting*?" Maribel said when they arrived in the banquet hall ahead of Max and Ava, who'd stayed back for more photos.

"It is." Jordan bit her lower lip and canted her head. "Pretty soon that ribbon...well, it won't look like a ribbon."

Maribel reached for Jordan's arm. "Don't panic. I'm sure it can be fixed."

"Actually, it looks more realistic." Jordan mused. "Have you ever seen doves take flight? It isn't pretty. Stuff happens. At least we won't have bird poop on our heads. I'll speak to the hotel staff and see if they can turn up the air conditioning. That ought to help."

"You're so...*calm*." Maribel studied Jordan as if she didn't trust that any minute now she'd burst into flames and there she stood without a fire extinguisher handy.

Jordan shimmied her shoulders. "I'm really enjoying this whole new zen vibe I've got going on."

"Hey! Jordan! Remember me? I'm Susan."

The little girl had run up to Jordan and stopped on a dime. Lucia walked behind Susan, apparently taking the assignment of everyone's nanny for the evening.

"I remember you, silly." Jordan patted the little girl's head. "You're one of my favorite people."

Her hair was wound in two pretty braids, adorned with bright pink bows. Jordan could picture Rafe braiding his daughter's hair. The total alpha dude might have been more at home with a son, but he'd fallen right into step. He'd have his jaw tight in deep concentration, fixing her hair with the hands of a man who'd dismantled bombs for a living. Braids were probably easy after that.

"C'mon, *mija*." Lucia offered her hand to Susan. "Let's go find our table."

Susan skipped away with a wave. They headed to the children's table with the Del Toro and Long nieces and nephews. Maribel followed them, making her way to the wedding party table at the head of the room.

"Hey."

A deep male voice from behind caused a tightening low in Jordan's belly. A warm masculine hand wrapped around her waist.

She turned and met soulful dark eyes that never failed to squeeze her heart. "There you are."

He took her hand and laced his fingers through hers. "It was a beautiful wedding."

"Yes." She couldn't look at him for long, the emotion in his gaze too jarring. "I'm happy for them."

"You know what I was thinking?" He leaned in, his voice soft near her neck, nearly a whisper.

"The same thing I was?"

"That could have been us."

"I know."

"Give me another chance."

"What makes you think I'm not?"

"Instinct." He shrugged. "I realize I'm not easy."

She gave him a smirk. "Our trip to San Antonio would suggest otherwise."

She reached and brushed imaginary lint off his shoulder. Face it, she just wanted to touch the black double-breasted suit he wore so well.

He fought a smile, rubbing the back of his neck. "That part has never been difficult for us, has it?"

"Never."

A quiet moment passed between them, soft with memories.

"Rafe!" Cole clapped a hand on Rafe's back. "Hey, listen, we're planning something for Max."

Before Rafe got spirited away, Jordan hissed, "Don't let them do anything stupid."

Rafe nodded and gave her a thumbs-up.

Chapter Twenty-One

The hall began to fill, guests arriving and finding their tables. Ava's parents were hosting an open bar and the "celebrating" was in full swing. It appeared that if Jordan had any work to do tonight, it would be with the "wives of the Long doctors," who were already heartily indulging in matching twin Cosmos. She'd keep an eye on that situation. But so far, no wardrobe malfunctions, thank goodness. All parts of the pregnant and buxom Valerie stayed firmly inside her dress. Check!

On arriving, Jordan conferred with the staff, the caterers and the DJ. Check, check, check. Every wedding favor on each table had a silver and *blue* ribbon. Check. The ice sculpture continued to melt away, but the wonderful thing was that no one cared.

Finally, Max and Ava entered the hall and were announced by the DJ as "Mr. and Mrs. Del Toro" to great applause.

"Sit back and enjoy, okay?" Valerie said from the wedding party table when Jordan took a seat next to her. "You worked hard but this is your brother's night. Celebrate with him."

"Thank you, I will." The hotel had assigned someone to oversee since Jordan was also a bridesmaid, so she forced herself to relax when the festivities began.

The first dance was to "Perfect" by Ed Sheeran.

But just as everyone in the room appeared on the verge of tears, the song ended and segued right into "Colombia, Mi Encanto." Ava and Max went into a clearly choreographed number. As they danced together, their steps together perfectly in time, Jordan wasn't the only one who gasped in delight.

Maribel covered her eyes. "Please tell me he's not making a fool out of himself."

"Not even a little bit." Jordan lowered Maribel's hand.

Max then urged everyone else to join them on the dance floor and before long the music was the pure beat of everyone's joy. Later on, when Rafe offered the first toast, Jordan took a sip of champagne on a mostly empty stomach.

"To Max, the grumpiest grump of all my friends, and also the most logical. He might have made a checklist for his future wife, but at least the genius recognized Ava when she stepped right in his line of sight. Ava, you're the best thing to happen to this frogman." He clasped Max's shoulder, who gave him a wry smile. "And Ava, just so you know, once a SEAL has you in his scope, he'll never let you go."

"No, he had better not." Dr. Long, the father, laughed from a nearby table.

"Oh, Daddy!" Ava laughed and waved him away.

Valerie's toast started with what one might expect from a third grade teacher. Obviously practiced at public speaking, she spoke easily and affectionately about Ava.

"When I first met Ava, she'd bustled into the Salty Dog to announce the Mr. Charming contest. 'Hey, what's "Mr. Charming?"' I asked. She was way too excited to tell me all about it!"

There was general laughter from the crowd.

"That's our Ava!" someone shouted, holding up a glass.

"But seriously, when it comes to a true friend by your side, having your back, you can't do better than Ava Long. She quickly became *my* best friend, and I couldn't live without her now." Valerie choked on the last word. "Sorry, I didn't think I would cry."

A general "aw" swept through the crowd and Ava stood to hug Valerie.

Once the DJ started pumping all the hip-hop music through the speakers, the dancing began in earnest. Even members of the Almost Dead Poet Society, who were doing their best to keep up with thumping bass lines. Eventually, the DJ switched to some upbeat country music tunes, and the dance floor became crowded elbow to elbow.

"Dance?" Rafe appeared at her side.

"Sure."

"You can thank me later," Rafe said, as he spun Jordan around the dance floor.

"For what?"

He lowered his head and the warm breath on her neck sent a sharp tingle. "The men thought it would be funny to decorate a bowling ball with Ava's name and link it to a chain. The old ball and chain gag."

"Oh my God. Whose bright idea was this?"

"One of her brothers. To be fair, they *had* planned it for the famously interrupted bachelor party. For physicians, once those guys get going…watch out. And I thought I would need to worry about the SEAL team."

"You talked them out of it. Thank you." She pressed her hand to his chest.

"Well, as I said, you can thank me later." He winked.

She tilted her head. "And how do you expect me to *thank* you?"

"Get your mind out of the gutter. You can go on a date with me tomorrow."

She still had to check in with her assistant and get a rundown on next week. A business owner could never truly be on vacation, and she'd combined hers with work. She had to face facts. Her sister was right: Jordan had become a bit of a workaholic. But her flight wasn't for two more days because Maribel had talked her into trying to relax a little after the wedding. Thank goodness for her sister. Jordan wasn't ready to say *goodbye* to Rafe.

"Where are we going?"

"The beach. For a picnic." No sooner did he utter the words than a bright flash of blond collided with his legs.

"Ooof," Rafe said.

"Daddy! Dance with me. I'm really good at dancing. Look." She twirled in a circle and held her arms above her like a ballerina. "See?"

"You should take dancing lessons," Jordan said.

"We'll sign you up, Shortie." Rafe placed his big warm hand on Susan's head, and she tilted her face upright. "When we get back to Dallas."

Yes, because of course, they were going back to *Dallas*. And Liz. This way they could all happily co-parent together. Jordan would go home to California, where presumably by now ever-efficient Geoff would have ordered his secretary to send over a box of anything she'd left at his place. Then she'd be alone again, working too hard, but now missing Rafe. Remembering the night he'd searched everywhere for her planner and talked her off the metaphorical ledge. The planner he'd bought to replace it and written in first. Their road trip and sensual night in San Antonio.

Of course, she and Rafe would text and call every day from now on. Probably. He might be able to get away but not often. Eventually, they'd both get tired of being alone and this tenuous new beginning would shatter. The thought made her stomach roil. She didn't know whom she was kidding. Losing him would hurt worse this time because now she understood what they'd had together was rare.

"Jordan?"

Apparently Rafe had asked her a question.

"What? I... I didn't hear that last part."

"What kind of sandwich do you want for our picnic tomorrow?"

It was now *their* picnic, because of course Susan would come. That only made sense. And he hadn't even waited for her answer. Just assumed she'd come. Susan's eyes were bright and expectant. And Jordan just couldn't say no to this little girl. In a short time, she'd burrowed into her heart with the utter faith of childhood. Susan had a child's heart and still believed in fairy tales.

Because she didn't yet know her father was the prince who became a toad.

But it was Rafe who made Jordan's final answer too easy. His eyes were solemn and deeply brown. He was trying so hard to get his old life back. All because he'd been far too honorable for his own good.

"Turkey sandwich, please."

The next morning, Jordan slept in for the first time in almost two weeks. She stretched under the cotton sheets and yawned, her tender feet sore and achy.

The wedding was over.

Done.

The event that had nearly ruled her life for the past year, as she wondered how she'd handle Rafe as best man, was finally completed.

Before the end of the reception, Max and Ava had left in a limo, on their way to spend the night at a Houston hotel near the airport. At the moment, they were probably on a plane headed to Paris, the bride's parents' wedding gift. As in Paris, *France.*

After the reception, the Long family had been effusive in their praise.

"Everything was absolutely perfect," Dr. Long, the mother, had said. "Down to the smallest detail."

Thankful for all the extra time and attention she'd spent on every detail, Jordan handed out plenty of business cards. The Dallas crowd of physician friends and colleagues of the Longs were equally impressed.

"Do you also handle retirement galas and anniversaries?" someone asked.

"Weddings are my specialty, but I do a little bit of everything."

"We have a lot of contacts, so we'll be sure to refer you, as long as you're willing to expand and bring some of your talents to Dallas," Dr. Long said.

Dallas. Right, the Long family lived in Dallas. Rafe and Susan lived in Dallas. But approximately one million other people also lived in Dallas. It was a huge city. She'd checked.

Dallas was a long way from Charming, Texas, but it was even farther from Santa Cruz, California. For the past few days, Jordan had spent far too many nights on her Google maps app, charting the distance between Charming and Dallas. Then Dallas and California, quite possibly getting ahead of herself.

Rafe had invited her on *a picnic*, not asked for her hand in marriage.

Because of Susan, he couldn't enter into any relationships that didn't have a good chance of success. They would both have to be fully committed. This meant Jordan would have to fully accept having *Liz* in her life, the so-called friend who'd snatched away and married Rafe for "practical" reasons. *Married.* They'd been married, no matter the reason, and that brought with it a certain kind of intimacy and commitment that he'd never had with Jordan.

Jordan reached for her phone to check in with Sherry.

"Hey, boss! How did the wedding of the year go?"

"I think it was some of my best work. You'd have been proud."

Jordan went over the litany of the near misses from the horrible violet ribbon to the narrow miss on the ball and chain joke.

"Who in the world thinks violet can replace blue?"

She was Jordan's right-hand woman for a reason. "Right?"

"Um, Jor, this is awkward, but…"

"Geoff?"

"He dropped by a few days ago, said you'd gotten upset because of the heat."

"Because of the *heat*?" Sounded like Geoff, unwilling to believe it would ever have anything to do with him. "I mean, yeah, sure, it is hot here. And let's not talk about the humidity. You should see my hair."

"Who cares about your hair? Tell me what happened with Geoff."

Jordan had never shared much information about her relationships. For all Sherry knew, Jordan and Geoff were perfect for each other. After all, Jordan had thought so, too, not long ago.

"It's not worth going into. We broke up."

"Oh, thank God!"

"Yeah?" Jordan laughed.

"No chance of reconciliation down the line?"

"Not even a little bit." Jordan would sooner end up alone.

"Maybe now I can tell you. I *hate* that guy."

Jordan was about to ask why when she remembered Geoff always pronounced Sherri's name as "cherry," like the fruit. No matter how many times he'd been corrected.

"You'll be happy to know I've secured us new business. We're going to be busy. I mean, you're going to be busy."

"You mean it? For real?"

Sherry might only be twenty-one, but she already had her degree, knowing exactly what she'd wanted to do all along.

"My sister might be a little bit right. Maybe…I've been working too hard."

"I'm glad you finally listened to someone."

She had, but not Maribel. Rafe had shown her that at the end of the day, she wasn't going to curl up at night with her sweet, hot, business plan. He'd been a detail-oriented, tough military man who now braided a little girl's hair, told fairy tales and located magic wands. He hadn't lost an ounce of his appeal and seemed to enjoy life more than he had before he'd become a father. Those tight lines around his mouth were relaxed and he smiled a lot more often.

"I'm taking the next two days as vacation, as planned, but call me if anything is urgent and needs my undivided attention."

"Don't worry, girl, I've got this!"

And for once, Jordan relaxed and believed this to be true.

Chapter Twenty-Two

Rafe had just finished wrapping up the second turkey sandwich when the doorbell rang.

"I'll get it." Valerie called out.

Rafe heard the door open and the sound Susan made when she squealed. "Mommy!"

Dammit. Rafe dropped everything to join everyone in the front room.

"I'm sorry to intrude," Liz said, setting Susan down. "I just missed my little munchkin so much. We decided to get away, and I thought, why not fly down. Susan just couldn't stop raving about this place. And really, it's *amazing*. What an adorable little town."

Liz was her usual take-no prisoners self, down to the cargo pants and work boots she wore. Tall and slender, she still kept her blond hair cut to just above her ears, as if she'd never left the military.

In a lot of ways, he thought maybe Liz never had. As a female helo pilot, she was rightfully proud of all she'd accomplished. Unfortunately, she never let anyone forget it.

Rafe made the introductions and Valerie gave Liz a quick tour of the lighthouse. While he paced downstairs, he checked his cell to see if Jordan had texted she was on her way. The last thing he wanted was for these two women to run into each other at this stage. He'd planned a lovely afternoon by the beach, not an ex-wife judging a new connection with his ex-girlfriend. Too many exes in one room.

By the time they all came downstairs, Susan had already clearly introduced Liz to Sub as well.

"This is the dog I want," Susan pointed. "*Just* like this."

"I see, and he's so cute, but we can't have a dog. We have Fatso. He's a big fat sissy and would be pretty scared of a big dog like Sub, don't you think?"

Valerie the teacher quirked a brow, and Rafe would guess it had to do with the *fat* and *sissy* reference. Liz would never be known for her diplomatic ways or choosing her words carefully.

"Aw, man!" Susan said, stomping her foot.

"Oh, *so* dramatic." Liz smiled and held out her hand for Susan. "Well, Carl is waiting for us back at the hotel. It was nice to meet you, Valerie."

"We were going on a picnic," Rafe interrupted.

Liz gave him the look that meant, *In your dreams, pal.*

"You come too, Mommy!" Susan pulled on her

hand. "My new friend Jordan that I told you about? She's coming to our picnic. You'll like her, she's *so* nice."

Rafe winced internally. He should have realized that Susan would mention Jordan in talks with her mother.

"I'm sure I will." Liz used her fake "happy" sing-song voice. "We thought we'd go to the boardwalk for cotton candy and rides, and I saw a bookstore in town that sells toys, too."

"Really?" Susan bounced up and down. "They have *toys*?"

Rafe resisted saying what he wanted because he refused to argue in front of Susan.

He simply smiled at Valerie and tipped back on his heels.

"I'll bring her back *after* dinner," Liz said without further explanation.

Only an argument would force her to reconsider. Rafe knew it was too late and he'd let it go. Liz had once more asserted her authority over Susan, and he was to fall in line and accept whatever morsels she'd be willing to throw him. He realized how lucky he was to get whatever time he did.

"Say goodbye to Daddy now," Liz said.

"See ya later, Shortie. We'll do the picnic tomorrow. Okay?"

Rafe squatted, and as Susan hugged him, he smiled into her hair and pressed a kiss.

"Bye, Daddy. Don't be lonely without me. I'll be

right back!" Susan skipped out the door, blessed with the blissful oblivion of childhood.

Valerie shut the door and leaned against it. "Wow. She's...*a lot*."

"Yeah." He lowered his gaze. "She is."

"Does she always do that, just barge right in and disrupt your plans?"

"Usually, I don't make it this easy for her, but this is your house and I have to respect that."

"I appreciate it, but I hate to see parents use a child as a pawn. Believe me, I see it enough."

"I'm sure you do. But this is the longest I've had Susan since the divorce. I'm not her biological father, and I also didn't adopt her. My rights are nonexistent, and Liz gives me what she does out of the kindness of her heart."

Of course, he didn't actually *believe* this. He rather thought Liz liked continuing to exert influence over him in some small way even after the divorce. And if she completely cut him off from Susan, she would lose that control. Liz might also appreciate the occasional respite from being a parent twenty-four seven, and with no extended family, all she had was Rafe.

"I doubt she does it out of kindness. She probably does it for Susan, or at least I hope so. Sometimes parents forget all that matters is what's best for the child. And you're good for her, Rafe."

"I like to think so."

Refusing to feel sorry for himself, Rafe finished

preparing the picnic now for two. The bright side was he'd have time alone with Jordan when he hadn't had nearly enough. That night on their way to San Antonio had been a gift. If he wanted her to give them another chance, at some point, she'd have to rediscover and remember who he was beyond a single father.

And so would he.

"Delicious sandwich," Jordan said, then took another bite.

Rafe smiled and squeezed her hand.

It was an ordinary sandwich, to be honest, but Rafe seemed distracted. He'd been sullen and subdued since she'd arrived today. Liz had surprised him by showing up for a short weekend getaway and taking Susan for the day. Jordan rather hoped he'd appreciate being alone with her, gifted this time together, but instead he'd gone quiet and introspective. Were she any other woman, and he any other man, she'd be worried that she'd done something to offend him, or the sizzle between them had fizzled.

Instead, this reminded her too much of the old days, when he'd return from a deployment unwilling or unable to talk beyond single-word answers. He'd hold her close, and she'd accept the lack of full sentences. They made up for it in other ways, with long nights spent in each other's arms, rediscovering intimacy. Then, she'd take whatever Rafe had to give. Weeks later, he'd be back to the man she knew and loved, just in time to leave for training.

But they no longer had *weeks*.

They were seated side by side enjoying the warm day on a flannel blanket she'd last seen on Valerie's couch. For once, the humidity wasn't oppressive, the wind welcome, and she felt comfortable in the short white sundress she'd borrowed from Maribel. She actually hadn't brought enough casual clothes for the trip. This time, she'd been smart enough to wear a floppy hat and stop worrying about her hair. It had long ago given up the ghost and was now one big and impossible wave.

Rafe settled them in a small cove far enough away from the lighthouse for privacy, but still on the house's strip of beach. They were mostly covered from the sun by a small tent that he'd fashioned, which served like an umbrella. Every now and then a light wind would whip through with a slight whistle.

"Gosh, it's such a beautiful day," she said with cheer.

"Yeah." He then leaned and pulled her into his arms, his front to her back.

"Well, despite all our issues putting it on, I thought the wedding was a smashing success. You would be surprised at how many of the Dallas people wanted my business card. Of course, that would be difficult to manage, long-distance and everything."

She felt his body tense.

"A Texas wedding was the exception for me, but hey, it can never hurt to have contacts in another area. Networking, right?"

"Sure." He lowered his head to her neck, kissed it, then lightly sank his teeth into her earlobe.

Sexy, oh hell yes, and her entire body buzzed with desire because Rafe never failed in this department. But out of one corner of her memory she also recognized what he'd done. He'd moved straight into "let's avoid talking about complicated feelings by getting naked."

"Okay, Rafe." She turned her body to face him, surprising herself. "We're not going to do *this* again."

"What?"

"Yeah, that." She pointed. "The one-word sentences. I don't have weeks to wait till you get past whatever is making you this tense and upset. And don't try to tell me everything is fine. I *know* you."

He lowered his head and studied her from under lowered lids. "Okay, that's fair."

"What's wrong?" She cupped his jaw with her hand.

"It could be a lot of things are wrong. Maybe the fact you just sounded as if there's no way you'll consider moving to Dallas, and I'm *stuck* in Dallas. Or maybe it's the fact Liz showed up unannounced, reminding me again who's the boss when it comes to our daughter. She showed up here, in a place where I'd finally found a little peace. When I want nothing more than to get away from her for as long as possible."

"Is she that bad?"

He quirked a brow.

"I mean, *I* don't like her, but I have my reasons. Still, she's Susan's mother, and will always be a part of your life. I've accepted that."

"You're amazing, you know?" He stroked her cheek.

"Yes, of course. I'm quite amazing and thank you for noticing."

He chuckled. "I'm glad you're okay with Liz because some days I'm not. But I signed up for this and she's Susan's mother. I respect her for that as much as I do for her service."

"Right. As long as we're being honest, there's something I…oh, never mind. It's not important."

"Tell me."

"The thing *about* Liz… I used to feel invisible around her. When I was with you, Travis and Liz, you three were close, with a bond and connection I couldn't possibly understand."

"We were soldiers in the same war. That was our connection. For me and Liz, it's about all we had in common. That and Travis. We both loved him."

"Regardless, when you and I were together, I belonged. But every time you'd come back, there was a gap between us that took weeks to bridge."

"We always did."

"Because I *made* it happen. I understood at least a little bit of what you were going through and how difficult it was when you came home. I saw it with Max, right in my own family. The adjustment for you guys is tough. I get it. But then, Travis… Well, all that happened. It broke your heart, and I didn't know how to fix that, or how long to wait for you to get past it. I somehow knew you never would."

"No."

"I'm sorry I let all of it come between us. All my jealousy and insecurities. My doubts. I somehow manifested my greatest fear, aside from losing you on the battlefield."

"What was that?"

"Liz would take you away from me. And she did."

"No. She never did." He reached for her hand and placed it on his heart. "This, right here, is something only you own. Always have, always will."

"Then don't shut me out." She crawled in his lap and ran fingers through his thick hair.

"I'm only trying to protect you. It's what I've always done."

"Well, no more. If we're going to work this time, it all has to be different."

His eyes seemed to brighten with a sparkle she recognized as hope. "Yeah?"

"You can't be the sun anymore. I have my own life. My business, friends, associates, my family. We're going to have to find a compromise."

"When you say words like that, I'll do anything to make this happen." His mouth slid down the strap of her dress to kiss a bare shoulder, then moved to her neck.

His touch was hot and solid, the slight scrape of his beard stubble against her sensitive skin. Her hand went under his shirt, luxuriating in his warm, taut skin. Rafe's weight pressed against hers and she lay on her back.

"God, I missed this," Rafe said, skimming hands under the skirt of her dress and up her legs in slow motions.

"Oh, Rafe, I missed you."

She framed his face in her hands, those soulful dark eyes tugging at a heavy sweetness in her heart.

His masculine mouth crushed against hers with slow and lazy, deep kisses. Torturing her. Slowly unwinding every single doubt. She couldn't let go of him, she couldn't pretend this didn't matter or didn't have to mean anything. This was nothing less than everything. He was everything.

"Don't worry. No one can see us," he said as he slowly lowered her panties.

"Are you sure?" she asked a little desperately, tugging at the waistband of his board shorts.

"Yes. But does it matter?" He gave her a slow, wicked grin and she nearly orgasmed then and there.

And for a long while there were no more sounds but her moans, mixing with the sounds of the waves.

Chapter Twenty-Three

When he was all of eighteen years old, Rafe Reyes had thought he might someday rule the world. Or, if not rule, at least help *run* it. And fine, not the whole world, just the United States of America. To *start*. Those were the thoughts of a young man filled with an unshakable, cocky spirit. The faith of a man who'd been born to a single mother of modest means who struggled to get by. He understood he'd never get anywhere except through hard work and unquestioning belief in himself.

He'd do better than his father did, and better than his father before him. He'd make his mother proud of him by getting his education, serving his country and eventually marrying the girl he'd loved since he was sixteen.

But one of the many things he'd learned about war was it blasted the hubris straight out of a man. He came back from each deployment no longer certain about winning a damn thing. No longer sure of anything. Waking up the next morning, limbs intact, was a triumph. Another day above ground. He hardly dared to ask for anything more.

But then he would come home, look into Jordan's shimmering eyes and see himself there. He'd remember who he really was and not the soldier he'd become. She'd gaze at him like he was...well, just as she'd said. Like the sun. He got addicted to that, the way she always made room for him. The simple way she'd let him know anything he needed would get done. She planned their future, set reminders; she organized based on his moves. His ambitions. They had a timeline for marriage, and it wouldn't happen until Rafe had achieved his military goals. She understood, or so he believed.

It had never even occurred to him that she'd had no real plans of her own other than to be a military wife. That, he knew quite well, could be a career in and of itself. A military wife was part of the team. But he'd never imagined how she might want more out of life than supporting him.

What an idiot he'd been.

He'd never noticed how she might have felt left out of that part of his world. This made sense because if anything, he'd worked to shield her from it. And paid for it dearly.

Now, sitting here at the Salty Dog Bar & Grill, waiting for Liz, he considered how much he'd allowed someone else to rule him. Simply because… she could. There were parental rights, of which he had none, but there was also doing the right thing on principle alone. Cutting off ties to the only father Susan had ever known would be wrong. And Liz was smart enough to know this.

A few minutes later, she strutted up to his booth, and he stood.

"Where's Susan?" she asked.

"I thought you and I should talk. Alone." He indicated for her to take a seat first.

Liz gave him a censuring look. "Is she with your *girlfriend*?"

"Jordan," he interrupted. "You *know* her name is Jordan."

Liz ignored that. "Because I've never left Susan alone with Carl. You and I had an agreement and I've respected it."

"Susan is hanging out with Valerie, whom you've already met. Jordan doesn't know anything about this meeting."

"Fine." She pulled out her cell and set it on the table. "What do you want to talk about?"

He eyed the phone, hoping she wouldn't start scrolling.

"I'm paying attention," she said, already on the defensive.

Not promising.

"I've thought long and hard about this and I think a move to California is in my best interest."

"Interesting. And this has nothing to do with Jordan."

"Of course it has something to do with her, but it's not everything. I've put you and Susan first—"

"Susan," she interrupted. "You've put *her* first."

"Thank you for realizing."

She shook her head slowly. "I had a feeling this would happen someday. You'd walk away from her because you want to start your own family."

"That's not what this is about." He refused to allow this discussion to turn into an argument.

Cool and calm. Keep it together, soldier.

"Then what is it about?"

"I haven't been back home to California for so much as a visit since we separated. I'm sure you haven't forgotten I have a mother who would love to see her only granddaughter."

"I knew it. This trip has made you arrogant. Now you think you can take Susan anywhere you'd like. Well, that's not going to happen, genius."

"It won't happen if you and I don't work together. But moving to California would be good for Susan. A new start in kindergarten. Watsonville is a small town, and we'd have the extended family support we've done without so far. Susan needs a larger circle. This could be a good thing."

"You want me to move, too? And Carl? So, then

we can be one happy dysfunctional family in the state known for dysfunction?"

He ignored the potshot against California, which Susan lovingly called "the left coast."

"I can't speak for Carl, but you could get a job anywhere in the state and you know it. There are defense contractors there, too. Big ones." He reached for Liz's hand and attempted to bridge the distance. They'd once been good friends, or so he thought. "For years, we've done things your way. You and Carl are happy, and I think that's great."

"Yeah, sure. You know what would have been great? If you even had the slightest regret or pain when I *cheated* on you. Even just a little fizz as all the air went out of our marriage would have been nice. Any hint of emotion from you would have been welcome."

"You can't say I didn't try." He let go of her hand. "I'm the only father Susan has ever known, and I will always love her like she's my own. She feels like my own. But I deserve to be happy."

"And you can't find a woman, *any* woman, in the entire city of Dallas?"

He gave her a long look. Liz knew he'd already found the woman. Found her a long time ago and then lost her.

"Think about it, Liz. And when we both get back to Dallas, we can talk again. The thing is, you should know I'm moving either way."

"What about your *daughter*?"

"That's why I'm asking you to work with me. I know you, Liz. Deep down you're reasonable and you want what's best for Susan. You lost the love of your life in that explosion and sometimes I think you're still allowing the shrapnel to stay in your orbit. Destroying every last piece of you. Maybe you wanted to be with me because I reminded you of Travis but we both know that didn't work."

"I lost the love of my life and I can't ever get him back. You at least get to have another chance with yours. How is that *fair*?"

"It's not, honey. It's not."

His heart split for Liz, who had lost even more than he had. But Rafe would balance the entire world on his shoulders if it was what he needed to do to get Jordan back.

And just maybe, after all, there was still the spirit of an arrogant young man hovering somewhere deep inside.

Jordan waltzed into the Salty Dog for lunch with Maribel before she had to grab her flight to California. The comforting scent of charbroiled burgers and French fries greeted her immediately. This little place already felt like home, and thank goodness Max and Cole had taken over the restaurant when it fell on tough times. Her brother, who'd been all over the world with the service, had found a home and community in this little beach town, so appropriately named.

They chose a booth near the front to enjoy a view of the boardwalk, the seawall and all the tourists strolling past, enjoying the gorgeous day.

Later, she'd see Rafe again. This time he and Susan wanted to hit the carnival rides one last time before they flew back to Dallas. Yesterday's picnic had been wonderful, and what happened *after* the picnic like something out of a beach romance. They'd cuddled and talked for hours about everything. They were careful not to make overreaching promises to each other. Long-distance was possible, sure. They'd done it before. But the important thing was Rafe wanted to come back to California. He'd promised he would find a way to make it work.

Debbie came and took their orders. Adam's newest menu item, an incredible goat cheese salad with grilled chicken, fresh-baked croutons, pecans and dried French onions for Jordan. Maribel chose one of the best charbroiled burgers on the menu, making Jordan immediately regret her choice. The smell alone was mouthwatering.

"I'll go back to 'watching what I eat,'" Maribel said and held up air quotes, "when I'm done with vacation."

"What do you think about coming back here again soon? We could visit Max."

"I'm in. There are those little cottages right on the beach. They rent them out, anything from one day to four weeks. And they're booked way in advance."

"I had planned to check into that." Jordan laughed.

"It's funny, I live in a beach town, too. But this is better in some ways. Even with all this humidity."

Maribel quirked a brow. "And closer to Rafe?"

"Dallas isn't *close*."

"Closer than California."

As usual, Maribel had read her mind. Yes, she thought as long as she was in Charming to see her brother, well…why not a little side trip to Dallas? She already had his address in her book. And if writing in her book hadn't been enough, yesterday had closed the deal. Rafe wanted her to come see him in Dallas as soon as possible so they could resume being naked together as often as possible.

As they were eating, Patsy and Lois from the Almost Dead Poet Society stopped by their booth on their way out.

"I just wanted to tell you, honey." Patsy patted Jordan's arm. "No hard feelings."

"About…?" Jordan said.

Patsy shook her head. "The poetry reading. I understand. It wasn't the right place or time."

"Sometimes we get a little overzealous," Lois said. "We do so love the written word."

Patsy nodded in agreement. "But nothing could compete with Max and Ava's little dance number. I happily relive it every day. Please tell me you got all of that on *film*."

Jordan chuckled. "Yes, the videographer did, but I'm fairly sure there are a few bootleg copies floating around out there. I saw both Cole and Adam whip out their phones."

"I think it was trending for a few hours," Maribel said. "They really weren't bad, not even *Max*."

No, not even Max, their somewhat grumpy older brother who apparently only needed a few classes to get the hang of dancing. Call it the overachiever in him.

"That's what they were doing every Tuesday night," Patsy said. "Took all the fun out of it when I learned *that*. I thought they were off engaging in a little premarital sex."

Lois elbowed Patsy with a shy giggle. "Oh, Patsy. Stop."

"Why? It's better than a makeover, mark my words. Sex is good for the complexion."

"Is it?" Jordan smoothed her cheek.

Patsy appraised her with sudden interest, making Jordan immediately lower her hand.

"You, my dear, are absolutely glowing. If I didn't know any better, I'd have to guess you've been having sex since the moment you arrived."

Maribel lowered her head with a smile, her shoulders shaking a little.

"Good to see you, ladies. Be sure to have some of the chocolate lava cake. Chocolate is a great antioxidant, too." Patsy waved and bustled off with Lois.

"Wow, I *really* like her. You heard her, right? She just gave me permission to eat cake. It would be an insult not to follow her advice. Listen to your elders,

I always say." Maribel studied the chalkboard above the bar with some of the daily specials.

"When do you *ever* say that?"

Jordan followed Maribel's gaze to the photo of a cake with a stream of chocolate flowing from the center like a river, little flames and a stick figure with a fork in his hand. "Yum!" it said in scripted letters.

At that moment Jordan's gaze landed on Rafe as he sat in a booth on the other side of the bar. With Liz. Even if Susan wasn't her mini-me, Jordan would recognize her anywhere. She was still gorgeously blonde and tall, practically statuesque. Slender and fit as always, probably still engaging in back-breaking P90X workouts. No one could deny that Liz was pretty, but she'd always had a tough and brittle edge.

"Is that who I think it is sitting over there with Rafe?" Maribel said.

"Yeah."

"What is *she* doing here?"

"She flew in yesterday, said she missed Susan."

"Or…she missed Rafe." Maribel scowled. "I don't like that woman."

A small thrum of fear and dread started in Jordan's windpipe and moved quickly to her stomach. "She's Susan's *mother*."

"That's not poor Susan's fault. I don't trust her mother and I never did. Sorry."

Now, Rafe took Liz's hand in his and his expression was…sweetly vulnerable. Almost pleading.

To take him back? To give them another chance?

Jordan swallowed thickly and lowered her head.

"Don't look, Jordan. That *jerk*."

"He isn't doing anything wrong."

"That you *know* of."

"I thought you liked Rafe."

"I do, but he's sitting over there, breaking bread with someone I *don't* trust."

"She's always going to be in his life, Maribel. It's called co-parenting."

"Gag me."

Well, time to be a grown-up. She wasn't going to cower over here in her booth and ignore them. Or leave in a huff. Or sneak out before they saw her. No. Because Rafe deserved the benefit of the doubt. He wasn't necessarily trying to hide this meeting from her just because he hadn't mentioned it. The thing to do was waltz right over there and say hello.

She stood. "Be right back."

"Wait." Maribel reached for Jordan's arm. "Where are you going?"

"To say hello."

Sure, it was the first time in more than five years that she'd seen Liz, but it was high time for a reunion between the two women who'd both loved Rafe.

Chapter Twenty-Four

Leaving her purse with Maribel, Jordan strode over to Rafe's table. "Hey, there, you two."

Rafe stood, and to his credit and Jordan's relief, he didn't look even slightly guilty. He threw his arm around Jordan's waist in a claiming gesture and gave her a light kiss on the lips.

"Liz, you remember Jordan." He gestured for her to sit on his side of the bench and waited for her.

"Hi, Liz." Jordan offered her hand across the table as she would any other professional.

Liz shook Jordan's hand with a tight smile. She'd never seen Liz look this uncertain, as if she wondered if Jordan would any minute now drag her outside for a cat fight. As if.

"Good to see you again. Susan couldn't stop talk-

ing about the wedding. She had such fun. I heard it
was lovely," Liz said.

"Thank you. I have to agree."

Rafe took Jordan's hand in his. "Liz and I were
discussing a few things away from little ears."

"That's right." Liz smiled, wider this time, like
she'd regained her footing in a tussle. "Our daughter
can be way too curious sometimes."

Our daughter. They have a daughter.

I remember, Liz. I was there too. And it's okay.

"She's such a sweet and smart little girl. You've
done such a wonderful job with her."

Liz blinked, her gaze flitting quickly to Rafe, then
back to Jordan. "Thank you."

In that swift and quick moment, Jordan recognized something that surprised her. *Liz* was the one
threatened here, not Jordan. She was no longer the
intimidated girl in awe of a helo pilot and Rafe's fellow soldier. Someone who understood everything
he'd been through. No battlefield here, no sir, just
three people whose lives had been altered by one
explosion thousands of miles away.

"Slide over," Maribel ordered Liz and then sat
next to her, forcing her to move. "What's up, you
guys?"

"Liz, you remember Maribel?" Rafe seemed to
be fighting a smile.

"Of course." This time Liz's smile was even more
strained. "Hello, there."

"Hey, long time no see. Did you guys already eat?

Because I'm going to order the lava cake, but I don't mind sharing."

"Sure, I'll have some," Jordan said.

"I'm not here to eat," Liz said. "And actually, I should go. Rafe and I are done talking for now."

"I hope we didn't interrupt the peace talks." Maribel chuckled.

"Not at all. It isn't anything we can resolve here. We'll take up the discussion again in Dallas once we all get home." With that, she reached for her bag, and turned toward Maribel.

After a moment, Maribel, who'd been scrolling through her phone, noticed. "Oh, you want me to *move*? Now?"

"Yes." This was said between gritted teeth. "Please."

"Fine." Maribel made a big show of moving as if the entire ordeal was the greatest of inconveniences. "Bye. Nice to see you again!"

"Maribel, what is your problem?" Jordan scolded as Liz walked away. "You're acting twelve."

"I don't like her. Sue me."

Jordan scooted toward Rafe. But instead of taking that as indication to move out of her way, he took it as an invitation, and tugged her closer. His hand slid high up her leg to her thigh.

"Rafe, move. Let me out."

"Why?" He narrowed his eyes.

It struck her how similar this was to the first time they'd sat together at the Salty Dog. So similar and yet separated by miles of emotional distance. Before, she'd wanted to get away from him.

Now she realized she'd probably interrupted a serious talk and guilt spliced through her. She should talk to Liz anyway. In private. They had a man between them, who would try to keep the peace, but sometimes it was the women who needed to chat.

"Just do it."

He quirked a brow.

"Please."

With narrowed eyes, he slid out of the booth and held out his hand for her. Jordan climbed out, then rushed out of the restaurant.

She found Liz by the driver's-side door of a silver BMW, scrolling through her phone.

"Liz!" Jordan called out, then walked briskly down the line of parked cars toward hers.

She lowered her phone. "Did I forget something?"

"No, I just wanted to talk."

"I'm late." Her tone was edgy as she clicked her key fob.

"It won't take long."

"Look, let me save you the trouble. I'm not sorry I married Rafe, but I'm sorry for how we hurt you. We honestly didn't mean to. How's that?"

Wow. Pretty damn insincere. Liz's bitterness still ran deep. She'd tried to replace Travis, not realizing she never could.

"Thanks for saying that, but I've owned up to my

part in all this…" Jordan waved her hands around. "Mess."

Liz quirked a brow. "Great. Now you probably want me to rearrange *my* life and move to California so you and Rafe can be together. But if you want to be with him, Jordan, if you truly love him, you'll move to Dallas. That's where Susan lives and where she has her preschool, babysitter and friends."

Jordan hesitated because Liz's argument was fairly convincing. Maybe Jordan hadn't been fair because this had been a difficult situation for all three of them.

Still, there was one thing that had to be said.

"And if you really love Susan, you'll give Rafe the same rights you would an adoptive father."

"Listen, however it happened, you love a man who has a daughter and an ex-wife to deal with now. If you love Rafe and Susan, make it easy for them both. Either walk away or make a commitment to uproot *your* life. Before you ask me to do the same."

"I'm *not* walking away. All I'm asking is, please don't cut Rafe out of Susan's life because of me. He needs her, and she needs him. No matter what the law says."

"Then I guess it's up to you to talk him into staying in Dallas to be near his daughter." With that, Liz got behind the wheel and drove out of the parking lot.

Later that day, Jordan spread her toes in the warm sand and leaned into Rafe's embrace. They were sitting side by side, watching Susan run along the surf with Sub.

After saying goodbye to Maribel and sending her on her way, she and Rafe had headed back to the lighthouse. They'd had a light dinner with Cole and Valerie and talked like old friends. The mood was light, except when she'd occasionally see a pained look in Rafe's eyes that pulled at her.

They were on a timeline and both knew it, though they'd resisted discussing it. It was nevertheless there, hanging between them, like a truth universally acknowledged. The sky is blue. Trees are green.

I'm going home tomorrow.

But they had one last day together before Jordan had to catch her flight back to California and resume her real life. This little swatch of time in Charming had been a gift. Because she didn't want the moments to end, she now wished she'd run straight into Rafe's arms the moment she'd laid eyes on him again in the bridal shop. But life didn't quite work that way, did it? Instead, it worked with steady, forward movements, if you were lucky, and a long series of compromises. Sometimes called "adulting."

Most days, being an adult wasn't a whole lot of fun.

But then, there were times like these.

"My fierce woman." Rafe whispered the words near her earlobe, then tugged on it with his teeth.

He'd heard the tail end of her somewhat heated exchange with Liz, having followed her outside. As

Liz drove off, Rafe had pulled Jordan into his arms and told her he loved her even more.

"I still don't get why she dislikes *me*," Jordan said now. "It should be the other way around."

Rafe went quiet for a moment, long enough for Jordan to know he had something to say.

"What?" She pushed against his shoulder.

"Probably because you were the third person in our marriage. I tried not to talk about you, but…she knew. After I came back from telling you we were getting married, she saw my reluctance to go through with my promise to her. She always knew how I felt about you, and eventually realized I'd never love her in the same way I loved you."

"Did you love her?"

"Of course. As a good friend, and the mother of my daughter. But I wanted to do better. I respect Liz even if we don't always see eye to eye."

"You both had a lot in common even before Susan."

Funny, it didn't hurt anymore to acknowledge this basic truth.

"Not enough." A light breeze kicked up, ruffling his hair.

She tucked herself into him against the wind, watching as Susan skipped along with Sub, holding her magic wand, singing loudly. Every few minutes she'd stop and throw a stick for Sub. If she thought it odd that Jordan and Rafe were hugging, she hadn't said anything. But something told Jordan that it wouldn't be long before she noticed. *Everything*. She was as bright a child as Jordan had ever met. It wouldn't be long before Susan had strong opinions about her world and Jordan's place in it. Susan was *really* the other woman in Rafe's life and always would be.

Rafe almost roughly pulled her close and pressed a kiss against her temple. "Come to Dallas with me. I love you, Jordan."

"I love you, too, but I can't uproot my life. You can't ask me to do that. I have a house and a business. My whole life is in California."

"We can work it out."

"How? Liz isn't going to make it possible for you to move."

"Yeah." Rafe kept quiet for a beat. "Well, I had to try."

Even if Susan was really the only one keeping him in Texas, Jordan couldn't call up an ounce of resentment for the little girl. She needed her father, even if Jordan needed him, too. A nearly impossible situation. Her breath caught every time she thought of going back home without Rafe. Missing him. Text messages and phone calls wouldn't replace being held in his powerful arms.

"Let's not make any promises this time, okay? No plans."

He quirked a brow. "*You?* No plans? Are you feeling all right?"

"Ha." She made a face. "You were right and so

was John Lennon. Life is what happens while you're busy making other plans. How about a guideline instead?"

"I like that. Now you're speaking my language."

"You are a prince!" Susan touched Rafe's head with her wand. "Aaand you are a princess!"

"Thank you. I've always wanted to be a princess," Jordan said, trying to disentangle herself from Rafe.

But he wouldn't let her go, his warm hand continuing to tightly grip hers. Sub barked a few feet away from them, the surf rolled in and out, and a seagull squawked in the distance.

And Susan *noticed*.

"Do you like my daddy?" she said to Jordan, tilting her head to the side.

"Yes, I do. Very much," Jordan said. "You know, he was my brother's best friend growing up."

"I have a best friend," Susan said, with the blessed distraction of childhood. "Her name is Jennifer. She always lets me take the first turn because she said she's my best friend."

"And I've told you that you can give her first turn, if you want her to *stay* your best friend," Rafe said, the hint of a smile in his voice.

"I know how to share." Susan bobbed her head up and down.

Interesting choice of words there, even if she was talking about toys and video games.

"That's good," Jordan said. "So do I."

When she glanced at Rafe, he wore the hint of a

smile on his lips, but not a speck of humor in those dark and deep eyes. Those eyes were about to break her heart. Sad, puppy dog eyes that made her heart squeeze and thrum painfully in her chest. She didn't want to leave him, but there was no practical solution. And even her new, more relaxed attitude didn't change the fact she had a paid one-way ticket home.

They stayed outside until the sun set over the horizon in swaths of red and gold. After some more splashing and jumping near the surf, Susan came to Rafe, kicking out her leg.

"Daddy, my pants are all watery."

"C'mere." Rafe grabbed a towel and Susan settled down on his lap.

Sub plopped next to them with a sigh, tired of all the stick chasing.

And Rafe held both of them, Susan and Jordan, as they watched the waves roll in and out hypnotically.

"I feel like the luckiest man alive," he said, and Jordan's heart tugged.

This was all she'd wanted, too. The man she loved and their precious child. In this case, the child wasn't her own, but it didn't feel that way. It felt like Jordan could never possibly love a child more than she already did Susan. She became quiet and eventually fell asleep in Rafe's arms. So she did have an off switch. Good to know.

"It's been a long day," Rafe said, smoothing Susan's hair. "She's wiped out."

Jordan cuddled closer to Rafe. "Have I told you how much I love you?"

"Yeah, but I can never hear it enough."

"I don't want to go, baby, but I have to." She hesitated for a beat. "Will you take me to the airport?"

"I don't want to, but I will." He then kissed her, the talented man, multitasking like a pro. "It's not always like this. I don't have Susan all the time. And when I do, well, we can get creative. My bedroom door has a lock that works quite well."

She heard the sensual tone in his raspy, deep voice and her body buzzed with desire.

"Noted. But this is fine. I don't mind this at all."

And they sat quietly to watch the black velvet sky sprinkled with stars.

Chapter Twenty-Five

Rafe understood that taking Jordan to the airport would be as pleasant as bloodletting. But he hadn't expected his chest to actually hurt, signaling the possible early onset of a heart attack. Or maybe a stroke.

Sometimes it was tough to work in the medical field.

Goodbyes at the airport were no longer the quaint and long exchanges of lovers kissing and embracing witnessed in all the romantic movies that ended with the airport scene. That couldn't happen at the drop-off curb where vehicles had time only to unload and be on their way.

Jordan made the unilateral decision that he should drop her off at the curbside because she hated goodbyes and didn't want to cry. Susan was strapped into

Jordan's rental sedan with them, and Rafe agreed. Taking a child through the airport should only be done when absolutely necessary.

He didn't like the idea of this quick adios, but they'd essentially said goodbye last night after he'd laid Susan down to sleep on the bed. Demonstrating his creativity, he'd found a private nook on the beach, and they'd made love one last time.

One last time. He didn't want to believe it to be the last time, but no promises would be made. This made sense for two people who lived several states apart. The only one he'd made was that he'd love her until the day they put him in the ground. If that had to be done long-distance, so be it. He'd love her until she got tired of him because he'd never again settle for less.

The next few weeks and months would involve the lonely nights and weekends he didn't look forward to resuming. At least he could throw himself into his work. And he had Susan, of course. Some of the time. He'd take a cue from Jordan and start planning more weekend outings.

Susan had regaled them both with twenty questions on the way to the airport and slowed down only when they approached the drop-off.

"When are *we* going on the airplane? We've been here *forever.*"

"Soon, Shortie. Day after tomorrow."

Two more days until his vacation was over. He'd head back to work and a four-day, twenty-four-hour rotation. Susan would go back to Liz, resume preschool, and he wouldn't see his daughter again until his usual weekend.

Rafe pulled over in front of the correct airline and flipped on the hazard lights. "I'm going to help Jordan with her luggage. You stay here, Shortie. I'm not going anywhere."

He went about the task, mostly ignoring Jordan's attempts to help. This was a lot of baggage, pun intended, and he only let her take the light stuff. He found a cart and loaded them up. Four suitcases seemed overkill, but then again this was Jordan, who had planned for everything.

Except, he imagined, for this goodbye.

She started to push the cart, then turned to him one last time. "Talk to you soon."

"Yeah, let's do that. Call me."

But in the next moment she ran back to him and they were in each other's arms. He didn't give a damn about travelers staring. Just held her tight in his arms and lowered his head to the crook of her neck to once more smell her sweet Jordan scent. It was going to haunt him in his dreams.

She fisted his shirt, wetting it with her tears, and he didn't care. He simply palmed the back of her head, sinking his fingers into her hair, held her to his chest and let her cry.

"Oh, damn, I swore I wouldn't do this. I don't want to upset Susan."

"It's okay."

It was just like Jordan to be worried about Susan. Rafe loved her more every day for the way she'd

opened up her heart to Liz's daughter without a second thought.

"Okay." She pulled away and looked up at him
with wet eyes. Her nose was pink, her lips trembling.
"I'm going in now before we both get in trouble for
holding up the line."

Someone honked. Right. They were supposed to
be moving along.

She pulled away first, turning to push the cart,
and didn't look back once. This was probably for
the best.

"Goodbye, *cielito*," he said under his breath.

Somehow this felt like the end of them even as
he told himself it didn't have to be. The two of them
were, at best, a long shot. The statistics were against
them.

Rafe hopped in the rental and drove, rubbing his
tight chest. Susan was uncharacteristically quiet in
her car seat. On the way to the airport, she'd insisted
they all play I Spy With My Little Eye until Rafe
thought his eyes would cross.

"Daddy, are you sad?" Susan's voice sounded soft,
and damn it all, so grown-up.

She would be five next month. *Five.*

"Yeah, honey, I am a little sad."

"But why?"

"Because I'm going to miss my good friend." He
braced himself for twenty questions, latest edition,
shocked when they didn't come.

"That's like me, when my best friend Josie moved
away to Corado."

"Colorado," he corrected, and pinched the bridge of his nose.

"I missed her so, *so* much. I even cried. Then my teacher and Mommy said, don't worry, you'll find a new best friend. And I did! So don't be sad. You'll find a new friend."

Not like her.

"That's good advice."

This signaled amazing emotional growth in his daughter. She had just *empathized* with him. In that one moment, Rafe felt like Travis was sitting in the passenger seat, giving a nod and a thumbs-up. Thank you, pal.

You're welcome. Anything for you, Kelly. Thank you for saving my life. Sorry I wasn't there to save yours.

Rather than go straight to the lighthouse to start packing, Rafe took a detour and went to the Salty Dog. Inside, the mood was cheery and light, typical for a family establishment. Debbie greeted them kindly and took their orders. Chicken nuggets for Susan, a charbroiled "heart attack" burger for him.

Cole waved from behind the closed bar, where he appeared to be stocking. Some of the members of that weird poet society were sitting at a booth nearby and Mr. Fink waved at him. He'd been the one who'd claimed to have plenty of apps on his phone when they all came to babysit Susan.

Stacy came out from the back office, little Tennessee Rose on her hip.

She stopped by their booth. "Hey, you two. We

just came by to see Daddy and get lunch. We're on our way home now. Mommy has a book to finish."

The baby girl, practically the very image of Adam, cooed and smiled. She held out her arms for Rafe.

"Aw, you look a little like her daddy." Stacy handed the baby over to Rafe and he held her in his lap. "She likes you."

Damn, he wanted one. Tennessee was adorable, with her sweet baby scent and drooly smile. He missed those times with Susan. It was impossible to be too sad around a baby. They required all one's attention and emotional bandwidth. No room for self-pity, that was for sure.

"No Jordan today?" Stacy took a seat next to Susan.

"We dropped her off at the airport."

"Oh, I'm sorry I didn't get to say goodbye."

"That's enough holding the baby," Susan said. "You can give Tennessee back to her mommy."

Both he and Stacy chuckled at the obvious jealousy from a four-year-old, and Rafe handed over the baby, who then leaned toward her next favorite person, Susan.

After a few minutes, Stacy excused herself, saying she really had to get back to her book and the baby needed a nap.

"I used to nap when I was a baby. But now I'm all grown-up and I don't nap."

Stacy smiled kindly and tousled Susan's hair.

When they'd gone, Susan climbed on his side of

the booth, went on her knees and framed his face. "You're still sad."

"Yeah, honey, I am. But that's okay. Sometimes daddies get to be sad for a little while. I'll be fine."

"I should come live with you."

It sounded so mature that for a moment he couldn't speak, too choked up for words. She wanted to fix this. She wanted to take care of him. And it was time to get over himself. He didn't have the right to be gloomy in front of Susan. She would take it personally, since she didn't yet understand the larger world, the one in which she wasn't always the center.

The universe in which adults screwed up their own lives and then had to live with the consequences.

"No, I don't think so. That's not a good idea. Mommy would miss you too much."

"But I don't want you to be *sad*."

"Me, either." He waited a beat, then held up his wiggling fingers. "And no one can be sad when the tickle monster is here."

"Oh, Daddy!" She squealed with laughter and jumped away from the tickles.

With that, he moved on, and went back to the business of parenting, shattered heart and all.

Turn back. Turn back.

Jordan checked her baggage and took her place in the long line. She pulled out her plastic bags of makeup and contact lens solution, set her electronics in the bins, and tried to ignore the incessant, loud chant in her ears.

Go back to him.
C'mon, you dummy!
Who leaves that kind of man behind? Who?

She did, because for God's sake, one didn't just drop their entire *life* for a man. Even if he was *the* man, who had already shown her he'd be a model father for her own children. She didn't have to guess at this, she'd witnessed it up close and personal. He *was* a good father. A father who put his daughter first, because did she really want a man who would leave his daughter behind for a woman? No, of *course* not.

And yet…and yet…she had plans and staying with Rafe was the definition of flying by the seat of her pants. But everything couldn't always go according to plan. She'd learned that lesson for the last time. But once you had a plan, you followed it, damn it. Until something went wrong. Then readjust accordingly.

She passed the inspection at TSA and lugged her carry-on toward her gate. Two hours early, because that was how she rolled. Something *could* go wrong, after all.

Or…everything.

She'd already lost Rafe once because of a stupid, snap decision based on her own fears and insecurities. She couldn't get past the pebble in her throat that told her she was about to make another mistake. Still, she had a work schedule. Plans that couldn't be easily broken. An airline ticket, for instance. Now that she was adulting, she understood this on a core level. A grown-up didn't just drop everything to go after what they wanted just because she wanted it. She wasn't four, after all.

But for the love of my life? Shouldn't he be an exception?

God help her, the thought of *Liz* and Travis, of all people, came unbidden. Had they any idea that they would have such a short time together, what would they have done differently? And poor Travis. He would have much preferred, if the choice was given to him, to be a stay-at-home father than a hero posthumously awarded the medal of honor. Of this she was certain.

Because no one was guaranteed tomorrow, no matter how many *plans* they made.

Jordan went up to the ticket counter. "Excuse me, ma'am. How hard would it be to change my ticket now?"

"We're boarding in ninety minutes."

"Yes, I know. I got here early." Jordan took a deep breath. "But…um, something came up."

"Well, at least you showed." Her fingers flew across the keyboard. "You have no idea how many passengers miss their flights, not accounting for baggage check-in and TSA lines."

Oh, dear God, her luggage!

"When would you like to reschedule?" Tap, tap, tap went the keyboard. "We have room on tomorrow's flight."

One week? Two weeks? Three?

"I… I don't know."

The woman stared at her blankly. "What do you mean you don't *know*?"

"I don't know," Jordan said with absolute wonder. "I mean, I *actually* don't know."

"Well, then, I can't help you, can I?"

"Can you reroute me to Dallas?"

Several more clicks on her keyboard while the agent muttered softly, "My, my, my. *Someone* can't make up her mind where she wants to be."

"It's just that plans change. And I didn't expect *this*, okay? Sometimes stuff happens, and you have to go with it. I *always* have a plan, but I haven't been necessarily happy, you know? So I'm thinking, why not try this? Yes, it's completely unexpected, but can you really *help* who you love?"

The woman quirked a brow. "*Yes*, I can get you on a flight to Dallas."

Oh, right. She was spilling her guts to this poor woman.

"Let's do it."

It took a while longer to get her checked luggage back from very annoyed clerks and then Jordan ordered a Lyft.

"Welcome to Texas!" said the driver cheerfully as he loaded her suitcases.

"Thanks, it's not my first time. I never left the airport."

"Did you forget something?"

"Yes."

They caught a little traffic but approximately forty-five minutes later, Jordan was back to the Salty

Dog. It was as good a place as any to begin, because she would need someone to take her luggage…somewhere. From what she'd seen while here, many of the people she'd met tended to hang out in the restaurant. She had to find a place to stay and they'd know someone. She couldn't stay at the lighthouse with Rafe, and she'd already given up her hotel room. Her only real plan was to fly to Dallas in two days. With Rafe and Susan.

We'll figure it out, Rafe had said.

She'd walk inside, grab an iced tea and text Rafe that she'd never left the airport.

A man kindly held the door open for her, helping with her suitcases, and she walked inside. She stood by the door, the sounds of chatter, glasses clinking and food frying a comfort to her senses. But only one person in the room caught her full attention.

Rafe stood from a booth near the front and slipped his wallet into his back pocket. He looked tired and a little…worn. He ran a hand through his hair and took Susan's hand. Then he turned to the door and saw Jordan. His expression went from the furrowed brow of confusion to the wide eyes of surprise.

And when he smiled, her heart cracked wide open.

There was nothing else to do but run to him, which she did, straight into his arms. He caught her easily and lifted her off her feet.

"I love you, I love you, I love you," Jordan whispered into Rafe's warm neck. "And I'm never letting you go again. You're going to get so tired of me."

"I don't think so," Rafe said and his voice was

rough. "That will never happen, but I look forward to you trying."

"Hi, Jordan," Susan said as if there was nothing unusual about this moment.

Rafe lowered Jordan and her feet touched the ground, but he didn't let go of the rest of her.

"I hope you don't mind but I'm coming home with you and your daddy for a little while." She glanced at Rafe and whispered, "We'll figure it out."

"Okay, because I want to show you my favorite park," Susan said. "And there's a fountain."

"I want to see that."

Rafe tugged Jordan's hand and nudged his chin toward the front door. "Looks like we have some luggage to take care of."

"Flying wild. I had only one plan—getting to Dallas. I already have my ticket. And I feel like I'm high on a trapeze trying to ride a bicycle for the first time."

He chuckled deep in his throat. "I'll be your net."

Then he took Susan's hand in one of his own and Jordan's hand in his other.

They walked outside, together, feeling very much like a family.

Epilogue

Six months later
Watsonville, California

"They're here."

Jordan rushed to open the front door of her parents' home. Her family had gathered together to celebrate her birthday, and tonight they had a special guest. Two, actually.

She threw open the door and there stood Rafe, smiling, looking dark and roguishly handsome in black jeans and a matching button-up, sleeves rolled up. Next to him, Susan, so cute in her braids and party dress.

"Jordan!" Susan squealed and grabbed Jordan in a hug.

Rafe followed and embraced them both in the circle of his arms.

Though Jordan and Rafe split their time between Dallas and California, this visit made Susan's first. It had been several long months of adjustment as Liz became accustomed to Jordan being a part of their lives. But like building a foundation brick by brick, she gradually won Liz over. Looking back, she thought it might have been the moment Jordan agreed with Liz that Susan could not take off all her clothes and run through the fountain of her favorite park. Turned out, Liz greatly appreciated the support and the two women forged a quiet and calm partnership. Mistakes were made. Forgiveness was offered and nobody was blameless.

Jordan acknowledged their whole situation had been tough for everyone. Even Liz. She'd lost the love of her life and in her grief reached out to Rafe. And at the time she had, he was single.

On Jordan's second visit to Dallas, Liz invited her to Susan's new school to meet the teachers.

Jordan regularly took every opportunity she found, big or small, to agree and support Liz. Jordan managed to convince her that she had no desire to take her place and she simply wanted to support both Liz and Rafe. So, at some point, they'd become a mutual society of three people who only wanted the best for one precious little girl. And Jordan promised that when she and Rafe had their own child, someday, they wouldn't treat Susan any differently.

Liz's eyes had teared up, leading Jordan to realize this had been a huge worry. She wondered whether or not Rafe would love his biological child more than her little girl and whether Susan would be left behind. Not a chance.

And good thing they'd discussed this because yes, *that* was happening. A little soon, and not exactly expected. Simply life's latest hilarious misstep. *Think you can make plans? Ha! We'll show you.* Jordan was six weeks pregnant, and they'd announce it to her family soon. *After* they told Susan.

Rafe had been ecstatic, his eyes full of tears when she'd given him the news.

"You'll marry me, of course."

"Is that a proposal?"

"Just wait. It's going to be epic."

While she waited for that moment, she would enjoy tonight's celebration. The family home was full to the brim with Max, Ava, the rest of her brothers, their wives, children, Maribel and Rafe's mother.

"Sit over here next to me, *mija*," Mrs. Reyes said to Susan, offering her hand.

Grandma and granddaughter had a special bond.

"What took you so long?" said Jordan's father as he clapped Rafe on the back.

"Traffic from San Jose," Rafe answered, then kissed Jordan's mother's cheek. He went down the line, shaking Max's hand, then Lou's, and greeting everyone else.

Yes, all was forgiven. Rafe had been accepted

back into the family like the lost son that found his way home again. The first time he'd had dinner with her family, they did everything but slaughter the fatted calf to celebrate his return to the fold.

Tonight would be a bit more low-key but still something to celebrate with Spanish dishes her mother and father had slaved over all day. The birthday cake was the one her mother baked every year for Jordan. Her favorite, pineapple upside down cake.

Susan kicked her legs under the table and seemed particularly animated tonight. Probably all the excitement of her first visit, and Jordan's birthday. And all this before any sugar.

"Daddy, can we do it now? Please?"

"Hang on, Shortie. Maybe we should wait until after the birthday cake?"

"Wait for what?" Jordan put her fork down. "Did you guys get me a gift?"

"Yes!" Susan squealed. "It's really—"

Rafe gently put a hand over her mouth and smiled. "No hints."

"You better do it now," Max said from next to Ava. "She's not going to keep it inside for long."

"She's about to blow." Maribel laughed.

"You're right." Rafe stood. "All right, let's do this."

"Do what?" Jordan asked.

But no one answered. Instead, they all watched as Rafe and Susan walked hand in hand toward Jordan's seat at the table.

"I'm ready," Susan said.

"What's up?" Jordan smiled as Susan approached.

Susan looked up at Rafe as if for instruction, then fixed her eyes on Jordan. "Um, Jordan? I have to…" She glanced up at Rafe again. "Ask you a question?"

"Yes?" Jordan laughed, not having any idea where this was going.

The last time Jordan had been in Dallas on Susan's weekend with Rafe, Susan had decided they'd have a scavenger hunt. They were to look for mermaids. She was forever coming up with silly ideas for games.

"Would you marry my daddy?" After a nudge from Rafe, she added, "Please?"

From around the family table came a collective rumble of approval.

Then Rafe went to his knees, holding a small black box he'd pulled from his pocket. Jordan covered her mouth, tears already filling her eyes.

"And there's a ring!" Susan squealed. "It's really shiny."

"Shh. This is my part." He grinned and stilled Susan with a hand on her shoulder.

"Jordan, I've loved you for what feels like my whole life. We've been through many ups and downs but always found our way back to each other. I want us to spend the rest of our lives together, and Shortie here has given her blessing. What do you say, *cielito*? Marry me?"

"Marry *us*!" Susan said.

"Yes, yes. I will."

Jordan stood and pulled Rafe up. She kissed him then to the sounds of applause and cheers from her family. Everyone here, together, watching the moment she'd dreamed of for years.

"Yay!" Susan hopped up and down. "She said yes."

"And now, let's have cake!" her mother announced.

Because, as if the proposal wasn't enough, this was her birthday. She would never have a better one. After singing and eating cake, they all spilled outside to the patio strung with white fairy lights. Music drifted through the speakers and everyone danced to celebrate another year.

And soon, Susan would hear the news she'd waited for. A little brother or sister. A baby. Jordan's family would learn of the new baby who would join their family soon enough.

Dancing, Jordan clapped her hands and laughed at Susan, waving her arms from high on Rafe's shoulders. This was her family. Rafe and Susan, and soon another baby to bless them all.

Her family might not look anything like she'd originally planned, but it was hers all the same.

* * * * *

#2983 FORTUNE'S RUNAWAY BRIDE
The Fortunes of Texas: Hitting the Jackpot • by Allison Leigh

Isabel Banninger's fiancé is a two-timing jerk! Running out of her own wedding leads her straight into CEO Reeve Fortune's strong, very capable arms. Reeve is *so* not her type. But is he the perfect man to get this runaway bride to say "I do"?

#2984 SKYSCRAPERS TO GREENER PASTURES
Gallant Lake Stories • by Jo McNally

Web designer Olivia Carson hides her physical and emotional scars behind her isolated country life. Until a simple farmhouse remodel brings city-boy contractor Tony Vello crashing into her quiet world. They share similar past pain...and undeniable attraction. But will he stay once the job is done?

#2985 LOVE'S SECRET INGREDIENT
Love in the Valley • by Michele Dunaway

Nick Reilly adores Zoe Smith's famous chocolate chip cookies—and Zoe herself. He hides his billionaire status to get closer to the single mom. Even pretends to be her fiancé. But trading one fake identity for another is a recipe for disaster. Unless it saves Zoe's bakery *and* her guarded heart...

#2986 THE SOLDIER'S REFUGE
The Tuttle Sisters of Coho Cove • by Sabrina York

Football star Jax Stringfellow was the bane of Natalie Tuttle's high school existence. A traumatic military tour transformed her former crush from an arrogant, mean-spirited jock into a father figure for her nephews. But can the jaded TV producer trust her newfound connection with this kinder, gentler, *sexier* Jax?

#2987 THEIR ALL-STAR SUMMER
Sisters of Christmas Bay • by Kaylie Newell

Marley Carmichael is back in Christmas Bay, ready to make her baseball-announcing dreams come true. When a one-night stand with sexy minor-league star Owen Taylor ends with a surprise pregnancy, life *and* love throw her the biggest curveball yet!

#2988 A TASTE OF HOME
Sisterhood of Chocolate & Wine • by Anna James

Layla Williams is a spoiled princess—or so Wall Streeter turned EMT Shane Kavanaugh thought. But the captivating chef is so much more than he remembers. When her celebrated French restaurant is threatened by a hostile investor, he'll use all his business—and romance—skills to be the hometown hero Layla needs!

YOU CAN FIND MORE INFORMATION ON UPCOMING HARLEQUIN TITLES, FREE EXCERPTS AND MORE AT HARLEQUIN.COM.

HARLEQUIN
PLUS

Try the best multimedia subscription service for romance readers like you!

Read, Watch and Play.

Experience the easiest way to get the romance content you crave.

Start your **FREE TRIAL** at
www.harlequinplus.com/freetrial.